Echoes of DECEPTION

A MURDER MYSTERY BY

DINESH ARYA

This book is a work of fiction. Names, characters, places, and incidents are either products of the author's imagination or used fictitiously. Any resemblance to actual persons, living or dead, events, or locales is purely coincidental.

First Edition: December 2024
Printed in India

Printed at Print Plus Pvt. Ltd., Mumbai
Typeset in Adobe Garamond Pro

ISBN: 978-93-6070-939-6

Cover Design: Prajakta Sawant

STORYMIRROR
Stories that reflect you

Publisher: StoryMirror Infotech Pvt. Ltd.
Unit No-F/705, 7th Floor, Kailas Corporate Lounge,
Veer Savarkar Road, Vikhroli Park Site, Vikhroli West,
Mumbai-400079, Maharashtra.

Web: storymirror.com
Facebook: @storymirror
Instagram: @storymirror
Twitter: @story_mirror
Contact Us: marketing@storymirror.com

Dedication

This book is dedicated to my parents, who made me what I am.

And my wife and son who supported me during the story writing phase.

And two of my school teachers especially Mrs D'Souza and Frank Vaz.

Dramatics Persona

Helen Rodrigues Gulfanzo:

A charismatic and controversial Executive Assistant, whose mysterious death sets the novel's central conflict into motion.

Pratap Rao Singh:

A seasoned, determined Senior Police Inspector with an unshakable sense of justice and a personal mission to uncover the truth.

Shyam Maheshwari:

A morally conflicted Purchase Manager leading a double life, whose indiscretions are hidden beneath his professional facade.

Aniruddh Pant:

The new General Manager, thrust into leadership having an illicit relationship with Helen and confidant of the owners.

Keshav Nath Pandey (Pandey Ji):

A long-serving employee who knows the company's darkest secrets and stands at a crossroads between loyalty and survival.

Rohit Das Gupta:

A brash and entitled heir to a political dynasty, deeply involved with Helen and tangled in the web of her murder.

Patwardhan:

A quiet yet influential production foreman, silently controlling key processes including the laboratory while hiding resentments toward the company's management.

Raghav:

A shadowy figure with deep connections to the black market, holding valuable knowledge about the poison used to kill Helen.

Jeeva Rao:

An old employee superseded by Anirudh and exhibiting animosity towards Anirudh and Helen at regular intervals.

Shubodh Das Gupta:

A powerful politician, deeply involved in the web of corporate and political corruption. His manipulation and ruthless pragmatism expand the stakes in the story, intertwining politics and crime.

The Owners:

A faceless yet influential entity within the company, controlling events from the shadows. They are the ultimate power behind the systemic corruption.

Peter D'Souza:

Helen's father was deeply involved in the local fishing industry and, more significantly, in the illicit trade of exotic marine life and smuggling operations, drugs and illegal chemicals for the black market.

Chapter 1: Helen

"She is Dead. Helen is Dead." Shyam screamed.

His high-pitched voice rang through the conference hall cutting through almost all the business at hand. Eyes furtively locked on phones that were illegally on, absent-mindedly scrolling on the usual tasty gossip ware of social media froze and fingers magically stopped mid-way. The more diligent ones froze in their dedicated note-taking.

The air in the conference room hung heavy with disbelief as the realization dawned upon them all: she was dead.

They were all there dressed in their corporate finery, some trying to outdo the other. The others just being present there almost as if that in itself was a huge favour to their employer.

An employer who'd achieved no major brand status, existing in a shark-infested industry with cut-throat competition.

In this attempt to infuse a motivational surge into the veins of the company most of the employees have been invited to an offsite conference.

This is where Death visited. With its Cold intent leaving behind a lifeless calling card.

Shyam Maheshwari, the Purchase Manager broke the silence. His trembling voice declared her fate. Panic swept through the room like a chilling wind. Whispers rose to voices with questions and chaos emerged shaking them out of the initial shock and moving them into action.

Many rushed towards where she was sprawled on the round table at which she was seated. Others simply ran to exit the hall almost afraid that Death would be tempted to take a few more out of their rank and file.

In these situations, almost always, a few 'leaders' emerge out of nowhere. You'd have seen that in a traffic accident. In one moment, there is chaos and confusion. Just a few seconds after the accident a few people move. They either saw what happened or just jumped in and took control almost as if they knew exactly what to do.

It seemed that Shyam was that man at this moment.

Aniruddha Pant was the General Manager of the Company. He was a new incumbent on the job. Barely been in the position and was just about getting his hands dirty getting to know the job and his responsibilities. He was previously the company's Sales Manager, and he was promoted both out of turn and ahead of a more deserving candidate. But more of that later.

Aniruddha's face was drained of colour. He was both shocked and out of his depth. He had never been in a near panic situation ever before in his entire life. But then in a moment the gravity of the situation came down upon him and combined with the authority of his position he suggested to no one in particular, the idea of calling for help.

"Call for an ambulance." He urged loudly. Even though the grim truth was evident - it was too late. She had already slipped away, leaving behind a void that no ambulance could fill.

Death separates the Living from the Dead. Very few of the living venture close to the dead. And so, it was here in this conference room, that Helen lay dead on the table and except for Shyam no one came close to her, to touch her or even try and resuscitate her. They all came to look – but that was all. Strangely, she was also turning a shade of blue.

"No point in calling for an ambulance. She is dead and she has been poisoned. Can't you see? She's turning blue!" Shyam said.

Reluctantly, Aniruddha made a call to the police, his voice barely above a whisper. He told the operator the nature of the call and the location of the hotel where the dead body lay. He tried to maintain a calm that he didn't feel. His head was spinning, and his stomach was gurgling. His mind was filled with events that would unfold next. The Police, the press, the employees and then the board of the company.

Everyone was mulling around. Now they gathered in the groups that they all mixed with and dealt with on a day-to-day basis. The accountants were all together, the manufacturing guys and girls were all together – birds of the same feather they flocked together, as soon as the formality of 'sitting with others not from your daily work group' mode of the conference was off.

There is a funny way in which communication travels around in any organization. It's called the grapevine. There's no particular starting point. It can start from the top and it can start from the bottom. But once it begins it takes on a life form of its own that is sometimes staggering in proportion and deadly in content. Depending on who it is targeted at and who is the carrier of such content the effect of its potency is felt. Sometimes the grapevine's content is also harmless. Those die away quickly. Masala is the prime ingredient of any Indian curry and even here the spicier the Masala the better the curry. Or the Gossip, in this case!

There on the lawn adjoining the conference room and in the small groups that were talking, smoking, gossiping or some on their phones already – the grapevine was buzzing.

Of course, the hot topic of the hour was the dead woman, Helen.

She was a colourful character. Depending on the circles that you asked – She was a rising star in some and an inspiration in others. She was a determined professional who set targets in her personal life and achieved them by dint of sheer hard work. Ironically, she had made a lot of acquaintances, but hardly any worthy of being dubbed a Friendship. So these 'badges' that she'd earned from these groups were just that. They were the trophy badges that many in the corporate world worked for. Achievements. It was not a testimonial or even a close reflection of the truth.

Some – especially some of the women called her a loose, characterless woman with zero morals. These were those who dared not even consider doing whatever Helen did in her professional climbing the corporate ladder drill – not just in life but as a matter of course in her everyday life.

These very same women who were now huddled in groups speculating, gossiping – were whispering in their hushed tones.

"She was pregnant. I saw her test report." One whispered loud enough for everyone in her huddled group to hear.

"I asked her straight." Another said.

"What?" The curiosity gets the better of people when bits of gossip are floated around.

"She was glowing, one day when I came into work. So I asked her. Are you pregnant?"

"Is it that obvious?" Helen had asked her not to respond directly to a question, but to answer a question with another question.

Sometimes an adept reply such as this not only answers a question but gives rise to another!

Now that she was dead – anyone could say anything. And the rumour-mongering would only grow uglier, meaner and as vicious as it could ever get. Such was Helen's personality in the company. Either she was loved or she was hated.

Helen Rodrigues Gulfanzo was of Goan descent as the name would suggest. She was unmarried by choice and completely attached to her mother. Amongst the many things in life that she'd discovered in getting to her current position in this organization as Executive Assistant to General Manager, Helen had realized long ago that people could be told what they want to hear more than they want to find out using their capacities to deduce.

With an ailing mother to look after, she needed all her wits about her and some to make it through life. But she'd decided – she was not going to lose the battle. She would do whatever it took to ensure that her mother would get the best possible treatment for her Muscular Dystrophy. Her mother's condition demanded both treatment and additional help, as and when required, a budget that was way above Helen's current salary earnings alone.

When you are mentally aligned to the challenges that Life throws at you then you really don't hesitate to do whatever it takes. This was Helen's mental attitude. But then she was also quite the actor. Most people's life is reflected in their faces. Not exactly like a mirror? But you can see it if you look closely.

Helen was a beautiful woman. She ensured that her good looks were not lost in the challenges that life threw at her. So, she presented herself well at all times especially when she knew that it mattered a whole lot. If she smiled at you you'd never think for a second that this was a woman who'd faced the worst that life could throw at her without even a flinch.

She was a Tigress on the rampage when she donned the mantle of the seductress which she played to the hilt. Helen was not your average call girl or escort. She was sophisticated, suave, extraordinary and intelligent. She used her looks, her sexuality, and the power of the knowledge that she had over men to the maximum effect. There were not too many men who didn't succumb to her slightest move.

The moment this awareness dawned on her was the same time she began moving up the ranks of just an ordinary temp secretary to highly paid executive secretary levels. She was an ideal foil for any boss. She used every trick in the book to get what she wanted done for her boss. She could wangle an appointment with a difficult customer. She could get reports in from 'busy' execs. Get a booking in a crowded popular restaurant. She was efficiency par excellence. In these days when solutions to problems mattered, no one bothered too much about costs for a highly efficient problem solver. That is how Helen positioned herself and got paid for it.

The Grapevine had it that Helen was the person to go to if you wanted God to look the other way when you sinned!

Having said that, there was this soft side to Helen. She was extremely courteous to the people below her. She'd never pull rank on an office assistant, an intern or a junior company employee. She was polite to the waiters who came like bees to a flower when she was in a restaurant to serve her. She was a gracious lady. She attracted a lot of people who were in distress to her. She would tip the doorman, and the valet and win over these people with that beautiful smile of hers laced with a heartfelt Thank you. No one ever forgot her smile or her kindness.

She would give them whatever support she could. She'd never turn anyone away just because she could.

Helen never kept track of the number of people she helped out. She'd say that instead of putting it into the church offerings I help these people out with whatever I can.

Sirens sounded in the driveway to the lobby of the Hotel and in a matter of minutes, the massive batwing doors of the conference hall were thrown open by a man in a police official's uniform who reeked of authority in no small measure. He was followed by a handful of other policemen whose aura seemed to be extremely dependent on the man they followed.

A moustache that was twirled and kept propped up in place, an official issue police hat, carrying his pistol in its holster, a police officer's cane tucked under his arm – he walked in with a marked swagger and an eye that swept from end to end of the hall in a matter of seconds. He wasn't exceptionally tall but one look at him and you'd not fool around with him thinking that he wasn't all that tall! He had that no-nonsense aura about him.

Before he'd even moved ten feet into the hall, his eyes locked on what seemed to be the leader of this motley pack of confused, startled, scared headless people.

Without even asking for clarification, he moved in the direction of where Shyam was still positioned at the table upon which Helen had fallen dead. By now she was blue. Not just noticeably? But her skin had turned a shade of unmistakable blue.

"I'm Senior Police Inspector Pratap Rao Singh from the Lal Bagh Police Station." He said.

Shyam stood up immediately. Extended his hands and shook the policeman's offered hand.

"I'm Shyam Maheshwari," he said taking in the firm grip of the other man.

Without asking for anything more the Inspector asked Shyam, "What exactly happened here?"

"We are all gathered here for a company conference and this morning just as we were about to convene, Helen here," he absent-mindedly pointed to the dead woman, "just dropped dead," Shyam said.

"Poisoned." He further went on to state, even though he wasn't asked for an explanation about her death.

Senior Inspector Pratap Rao didn't bat an eyelid. He just turned around and told everyone to leave the room and told them to go into their respective rooms and stay there till he called for them, if necessary. He explained that they were not to leave the hotel under any circumstance without his express permission.

Pandey or Pandey Ji as he was commonly referred to amongst the company staff was one of the oldest serving employees in the organization. He was the Official Keeper of the Secrets. He was the Trusted One. He was the Eyes and the Ears of People who poured in the money to run this organization. Not many had even seen them, but Pandey ji spoke to them and interacted with them regularly.

He was seen shepherding the confused lot of employees out of the hall.

"You." The authority-ridden voice of the Senior Inspector rang out across the hall.

Almost everyone turned.

He waved a hand almost to everyone and no one in particular dismissing them all from his call, till his pointed fingers rested on one man.

Pandey ji.

"Ji Sir." Pandey ji said.

"I want you here". The Senior Inspector said. That was no request. There was no if you please. If you'd heard a command, then this was one.

Pandey ji moved towards the policeman and Shyam.

As he neared them, he heard the Senior Police Inspector tell Shyam, "You too may leave. I will be calling for you shortly."

Shyam was surprised. He thought he'd be asked to stay and offer his version. He wasn't used to being so summarily dismissed.

Senior Police Inspector Pratap Rao put his arm around Pandey Ji and steered him towards one of the round tables away from the body.

"Now, let's sit here you and I and tell me all that you have to tell me."

Pandey Ji was in a state of shock. Why was the policeman asking him of all the people in the organization? What did he want to know? He prayed fervently to Kal Vairabh, his family's resident deity in his hometown Balarampur in the state of Uttar Pradesh.

Don't let the Policeman hear the loudly thudding beat of his heart.

❑❑❑

Chapter 2: Pandey Ji

On a warm summer day in 1995, Keshav Nath Pandey said a tearful goodbye to his mother, brothers, and friends in Balarampur, Uttar Pradesh. His father had died in an accident when he was younger, leaving Keshav as the eldest son. He was heading to Bombay, Maharashtra, a city filled with promises of success but also stories of hardship. Many had made the journey before him, hoping for a better life, driven by poverty and desperation.

Life in these villages had become desolate. First, the young and strong left for the Army or Police. Then the craftsmen and farmers, whose lands were dry and unforgiving, followed, seeking jobs as gardeners in lush, urban gardens. Eventually, entire families left as men found work in cramped city tenements.

Keshav had seen others succeed, like Pramod Shastri, a village man who dropped out of school early but became a successful cook in South Bombay. However, Keshav had not acquired any real skills. He became a mediator in village disputes, earning respect but little income. With no real means of support, he too decided to head to Bombay, praying to his deity, Kal Bhairav, for success.

The journey from Balarampur to Bombay was arduous. Keshav boarded the Mail train from Gorakhpur in an unreserved compartment packed with hundreds of people. The heat was intense during the day, while the nights were cooler, but the suffocating air inside made it unbearable. The hope of a better future kept Keshav going as he resolved never to return home in such dire circumstances.

When the train finally reached Victoria Terminus, Keshav was hit by the overwhelming sights, sounds, and smells of the city. He covered his nose with the pink towel he carried, a constant companion on the journey, as he pushed through the crowds. After speaking with his uncle on the phone, he took a bus to Chembur, where he would begin his new life.

Living with his uncle was a humbling experience. They shared a small space with six other men, each working long hours and taking turns cooking and cleaning. Keshav quickly followed his uncle to work, where his uncle was a "Man Friday" for a wealthy family, handling everything except cooking. Seeing Keshav's willingness to help, the businessman offered him a job as a personal assistant. Keshav accepted it gratefully.

Keshav quickly adapted to his new role, becoming indispensable to the businessman and learning the art of navigating office politics. Over time, his proximity to power gave him influence, and he provided valuable insights to his employer about the inner workings of the company.

As the pharmaceutical company grew, Keshav's position solidified. He became a trusted confidant, his master's eyes and ears in the factory. He lived by the motto his master taught him: "To become valuable, add value." This trust and loyalty would shape Keshav's future in ways he never imagined.

Decades later, Keshav had built a comfortable life in Bombay, having integrated himself into a world far removed from his rural roots.

❑❑❑

Chapter 3: Senior Police Inspector Pratap Rao Singh

Pandey ji squirmed in the presence of the Senior Police Inspector. It was not just the physical aura that the police officer exuded but it was also that unwitting fear factor that occupied the minds of the average layman about the police in general. Most law-abiding public shuns the police almost as if the police carry a stay-away-from-us persona.

It was not an uncommon phenomenon. Particularly in Bombay, amongst other things, was also where crime festered on like an old wound that refused to heal. There was this rather unpredictable but palpable relationship between the underworld and the police. On some days the Police were in control of everything and at other times it seemed that the whole city was in the grip of the underworld.

The police – except the plainclothes police personnel – donned a uniform that would announce to anyone about their occupation. Keepers of the Law, a force by themselves. For the common man, the uniform itself was enough. It was for the police department – the rank and the hierarchy. Perhaps that is why – unlike in America – where the police force is armed to the teeth – the Indian policemen are barely armed, except for that baton.

During the COVID-19 pandemic when the whole country shut down, those who were foolish or brave – depending on which side your perspective was – who ventured out got a taste of that baton. The authorities displayed the grim results as vivid advertisements in support of the enforced Stay Indoors campaign.

Those who knew of this invincible but powerful combination of the uniform, and the fear factor, utilized it to the hilt. This 'power' was heady. It defined the swagger, the attitude, and a certain mindset, and even took on its own behavioural traits. Those who knew and those who existed as if in a mundane job were distinguishable in their differences as night is from day.

Senior Police Inspector Pratap Rao Singh was one of those who understood the power and wielded it to perfection.

That was what Pandey ji felt when he was beckoned rather unceremoniously towards the policeman on that memorable day when Helen had died.

"So," Pratap Rao Singh began draping an arm around Pandey ji's shoulders, "you seem to be well known by everyone. The manner in which you were herding people out of the hall – it looks like you know everyone here."

"Sir, I have been a loyal servant of this establishment and its owners for the past 30 years." Pandey Ji began defensively.

"That may be true, but the owners aren't here today, are they?" The Inspector asked him.

"No sir, they are not – but there are others here who are responsible officers and there are also staff – who manage this company. The owners come for important meetings and board meetings." Pandey Ji explained the owner's absence.

There was an uneasy silence that hung in the air. The Policeman was looking at Pandey Ji almost as if he'd made up his mind as to who the murderer was.

Pandey Ji's squirming became more evident. He had this habit of wringing his hands when he was overcome with a feeling of helplessness or when he was just uncomfortable in a particular situation.

"Where did you say you are from?" The Policeman asked him suddenly.

"Balarampur, UP." Pandey ji said

"Quite a long way from home, hey Pandey ji." The Policemen quizzed him. That level of scrutiny was making Pandey ji squirm even more.

"What to do, Sahib? I too have a family and where I come from, there's not much scope except to leave our hometown and seek employment in a faraway city like Bombay, I mean Mumbai." Pandey ji explained.

Like most old-timers it did take Pandey ji quite a while and some effort to refer to Bombay as Mumbai.

"Yeah, I understand that Pandey ji." The Policeman said in a much softer voice than he'd ever used with Pandey ji since the questioning began this morning.

"Come," The Police Inspector said, almost steering Pandey Ji towards the lawn.

"You see, like you, I am also an immigrant in a manner of speaking here." The Police Inspector said.

"My father moved here a long time back from Dehradun, where our family has been living for many centuries.".

"Really." Pandey ji said almost like that information was something that was of paramount importance.

" Yes. You see, I am the son of conservative parents, high on values. My father was an Arya Samaji and member of RSS. My mother was extremely kind and caring, she was a post-grad in home science. I had a very sickly childhood. Smallpox, diphtheria, and cervical spondylitis tormented me from age 2 until I turned 19. My father taught us the Purpose of Life, taught us the essentials of karmic living while my mother instilled in us the need to be caring towards others. My father was a multifaceted personality, good at sports, wrestling, photography, yoga, hypnosis, astrology, palmistry, you name it. Very high on curiosity and a great learner." The Police Inspector told Pandey ji.

Then after a pause, he added, "I picked up only hypnosis, astrology from him but my favourite is palmistry by a long shot."

'Could he read my mind? Is that what he was trying to tell me? I know what is happening inside your mind. That is why I called you.' These thoughts screamed silently inside Pandey Ji's head. Otherwise, why would the Inspector have to tell him – of all the people – all that he shared with him?

"Having said that Pandey ji, I believe in Karma. In my job I have seen human beings up close and personal and in addition to having studied human psychology I remain a seeker of truth and ultimate salvation. That is what I promise to uphold in my job." The Inspector continued as if there wasn't a pause.

'Is he saying that there are zero suspicions that he has about me?' Pandey ji wondered again silently to himself. He wished the Inspector could hear this question. It would help a great deal to know what was going on through the other man's mind.

"At the same time, the world to me is divided between three kinds of people, the evil, the good and the average. And I quite firmly believe that evil and good are God's ideas of this world. And except for a handful, nobody is completely good nor completely evil. Circumstances play a great role and can make a good man do bad things and vice versa." The Police Inspector continued as if he was talking to another philosopher friend in conversation over a cup of coffee.

Pandey Ji's mind was going to burst. He didn't understand anything of what the Police Inspector was saying. He didn't understand why he was telling him – Pandey Ji – of all the people in the company all these things when there were more important things at hand – especially the discovery of Helen madam's murderer.

"And you know what Pandey ji, my basic behaviour, though it is sceptical at times because of the job I am in – it is to look at the positive side of things." The Policeman said with a faint smile that raised his moustache a little more than it would have remained otherwise.

He lifted the hand that he had wrapped around Pandey ji's shoulder all this time and thumped his back almost as if to say – There I told you a lot about myself – things which I normally don't even reveal to my closest colleagues.

But he wasn't done just yet.

He continued walking with Pandey ji and from a distance it looked as if they were two old friends discussing the world, the weather or just about the times that they'd not seen each other over the years.

"As my trainer, Soli Doctor used to say – "Look for an opportunity in every calamity, not for a calamity in every situation. And so I have learnt valuable lessons and I have learnt many things having developed such an attitude." The Police Inspector told the now totally confused Pandey Ji. The latter had absolutely no clue as to why he was being told all this.

"That is why I came into the Police Force. To be able to mete out justice. To be able to absolve the underdog. To be looked upon as a Dispenser of True Justice. Not be swayed by the rich and the powerful. Not to be pushed down because the truth is too uncomfortable. I am Senior Police Inspector Pratap Rao Singh and I am not an accidental policeman, I didn't get here because I knew a certain politician who knew the DG who 'fitted' me into the system or any such thing as Pandey ji. Right now where I am standing in my life is the sum and substance of my entire Life's Dream. I have wanted to be here. I could have been anywhere else in this entire world. But my Destiny has summoned me here today to solve this murder and by God, I will do it if it's the last thing I will do." The policeman said almost as if that was the last layer of his multi-talented persona that he was just unravelling like a load of bricks on an unsuspecting listener.

He was waiting for this tedious introduction to conclude. He wanted to go back to the staff – especially the ones close to him in the management – tell them what happened and assure them that he'd done everything that was possible to manage the police.

"You know Pandey ji, I had an Anglo-Indian nursery teacher, her name was Ms. Daphne. She taught me these lines which I remember from back then – my childhood." The Police Inspector actually smiled as he recollected the song and sang a few lines from it.

"A smile is quite a funny thing, it wrinkles up your face, but when it's gone, you'll never find its secret hiding place. You smile at her, she smiles at you and so one smile makes two"

Something like that, I think if I remember right. But of course, you wouldn't know, would you Pandey ji." The Inspector smiled at his own pathetic joke and gave Pandey ji another one of his thumps on Pandey ji's unsuspecting back!

Abruptly he turned around and faced Pandey ji.

"Did Helen's murder make you lose your smile Pandey ji? Or were you expecting this for a while now? You know everything that goes on in this company, did you see this coming?" The question and the manner in which it was asked was so sudden and unexpected that Pandey ji could only blurt, "Sir she used to have a lot of things going on with a lot of men. Sometimes one of her partners would know that she was two-timing. Sometimes they didn't. There have been issues in the past because of Helen. She'd use her influence and her proximity with the management to get promotions made, promotions stalled, pay increased and pay stalled. She was a woman of many talents. Yes, sir, it was only a matter of time before one of her exploits got her into trouble."

The Inspector looked at Pandey ji right into his eyes.

"You see Pandey ji, do you realize now why I talked to you about my past and my upbringing and my parents and all that?" The Inspector asked Pandey ji.

"Sir I did wonder why you were telling me all that." Pandey ji shrugged effusively his shoulders indicating his complete non-comprehension about why he was told what he'd just heard.

"Now you think that I am a friend. You think you know me. You think that you can also tell me anything that is close to your heart. You see Pandey I just bypassed your logical thinking mind, I hypnotized you into believing in me. And you are someone who doesn't usually believe people so easily, do you?" The Inspector asked. Now his voice had taken on that understated menacing tone. He hadn't even raised his voice and Pandey ji knew instinctively that he'd just told the wrong man a lot and he was wondering if that would make him a suspect in the Policeman's eyes.

"Sir," Pandey ji looked back at the Inspector's eyes almost pleadingly, "I had nothing to do with Helen's death. You should ask the others. Especially ..." he said, jerking his head backwards indicating where the General Manager Anirudh Pant was hovering at a distance looking at the developments going on the lawn between Pandey Ji and the Senior Police Inspector.

"No, Pandey Ji, I don't think you have had anything to do with Helen's murder." The Police Inspector looked Pandey ji squarely in the eye. "However, please don't leave the hotel premises. I will need your help to call in more people. Please give me your mobile number and please wait for my call." The Inspector told him.

Pandey Ji was visibly relieved. He let out a loud swoosh. That statement from the policeman was reassuring to Pandey Ji to no end.

Senior Police Inspector Pratap Rao Singh twirled his moustache absent-mindedly in deep thought. He knew about relationships a bit. He had just broken off his own relationship with a girl whom he thought he would marry. It wasn't easy to handle breakups. There was sadness, of course. But there was also anger. The Why Me, why did it have to happen to me syndrome. The long evenings and the empty tirades. The attempts at a patch-up. All your senses and your instincts come to the fore. You don't want to go down on your knees and beg her presence back in your life. That's just one half of you telling you so. The other half, the man who desperately needs to be loved and mollycoddled – wants you to do whatever it takes to bring her back. Then the male macho comes alive. You didn't even know existed lives within you. What if she took these reconciliatory and apologetic gestures as a sign of weakness and starts to dominate him in the future?

When he'd heard about a rumour that his ex had just been seen in public with another man, a wave of rage consumed him. He didn't see that coming either. Not trusting himself with his own service revolver, he kept it locked in his office cabinet safe when he went home, after duty. What if he got drunk and went to her home and shot her in the face? These were the nightmares of his liquor-induced drunken stupor that woke him up in the middle of the night. The cops coming to arrest him.

He'd chide himself. Nah! That was just a dream. You go back to sleep. Just sleep.

He shook his head. Sometimes one's own experiences taught one so much about navigating life.

He turned around and faced Pandey Ji again. Again, the heavy arm of the law was on Pandey ji's shoulder. Propelling him towards where Anirudh Pant was standing, almost where the lawn ended and where the tiled-covered alleyway to the swimming pool began, lowering his head to Pandey ji's ears he said in an almost theatrical conspiratorial whisper, "Please ask your General Manager to come to me. I am going back to the Conference Hall."

A completely relieved Pandey Ji almost ran to do exactly that.

❑❑❑

Chapter 4: The Affair

Helen was Executive Assistant to the General Manager, Aniruddh Pant. They worked very closely. She knew him than more than most people could ever fathom Aniruddh. It wasn't a mere knowing! That would indicate a superficial knowledge of a work colleague, or perhaps his working style.

This was much more intimate than that.

Helen realized very early on that the owners of the company had developed an implicit trust in Aniruddh much before he was anointed General Manager. That was confirmed the moment he was officially appointed, superseding someone else who was actually a better candidate than Aniruddh. Till then for Helen – Aniruddh was just another spoke in the wheel. Nothing more, nothing else.

When his ascension was announced with no other change in the organization's structure at that top level, Helen decided that she couldn't afford to let Aniruddh run the office of the General Manager on his own accord.

Thus that stalking leopard that she was, she moved in for the kill early. When a new person moves into an existing position there is a certain uncertainty about that person's next move despite his or her domain knowledge, understanding of the job per se or even their experience in managing peers and colleagues. She sensed that Aniruddh was testing his feet in new waters and that is how she made her first move.

She offered him her complete support. That meant that she would give him dossiers on various people in the organization. Either directly or indirectly connected with the General Manager. She knew each of these people. She knew about their character, she knew about their minor vices – who drank, who smoked and in some cases – she knew their major vices too. Whether someone had an illicit relationship with a co-worker, and most importantly – she knew who were the grapevine contributors and who pushed the grapevine buttons.

In short – she knew the system. The system knew of her. She didn't participate in the system stating her Non-Disclosure-Agreement as some powerful Bible upon which she'd sworn her confidential silence when she'd assumed office of Executive Assistant. In this company the Executive Assistant was not a 'mere job'. It carried unimaginable powers. It was a proximity to the who's who position. It was a position that assured the incumbent complete access to the most important information of the company. Combined with the character of someone like Helen the Power of the Position was truly awesome. She was the unwritten General Manager, the woman who had the General Manager's ears.

She secretly smiled when she'd heard such things whispered about her. Whisper because no one dared to accost Helen in the face with such unfounded truths. She'd crucify that person.

She smiled because if they only knew the truth was not the General Manager's ears she had but that she had him by his balls!

Aniruddh Pant was smitten hook line and sinker by the woman who was assigned to work for him.

It began very innocuously when she asked him to give her his laptop so that she could update some stuff for him. He was only too happy to have some support – especially the rather mundane but important secretarial aspects of his office.

By the time she'd returned the laptop back to Aniruddh she'd got a complete clue of his browsing history. He'd downloaded his WhatsApp account onto his laptop perhaps because that would give him access to his WhatsApp account without having to seem to be hanging on his phone, especially when he was 'working from home'.

So she saw who he was 'talking' to and gathered that Aniruddh was somewhat of a flirtatious character, but didn't have the balls to get into an affair because he knew his wife would skewer him if she'd ever got to know.

She saw the women whom he chatted up – made notes, made her own inferences of their character depending on their currently relationships – whether they were married or in a relationship with someone else – Helen ensured that whatever information she gathered was as close to the truth as is possible.

This 'getting the complete picture' exercise was important in Helen's mind because she figured that if she knew who she was dealing with she could administer the exact dosage, the kind of dosage and ensure that the 'victim' would never get out of her grasp.

At first she made vague references to the pop ups that came up randomly on his laptop when she was working on it. He nearly popped his eyes out in fright knowing he'd been caught with his hands in the cookie jar. But Aniruddh was a smooth operator and a habitual offender in such flirtatious matters. He tried to wing it out in his usual style.

What she did next baffled him. She didn't tell him that it was wrong to be cheating on his wife or try to give him a lecture on morals. In her position she could. But she told him something that would ensure that the fly walked into the spiders den. She said she understood the distractions because she understood the kind of work pressure he was under.

So he began to confide in her.

She encouraged him on and very soon in the middle of the office house Aniruddh would take a discreet call from one of his many 'friends' who just happened to be a woman who by the way 'reached out to him' for advice, counsel, or just plain camaraderie.

The next thing she did was to present herself to him in outfits that clamoured for attention. A buxom woman with an impressive figure, Helen knew the power of her assets. She flaunted it when she had to and she used it to the maximum effect when she needed to. Fatality was the result. No prisoners of war. No one left standing to tell a tale of I nearly fell into her grasp, but just victims.

And she was ruthless in her mission. Till she got what she wanted she didn't let go of the person. That could be man or woman. She didn't care. She'd have made a good Kamikaze pilot.

Her seduction was not ordinary. It was not your usual oomph. It was subtle. It was a hint. It was a look. It was a smile. It was just the brush of her oozing sexuality that hit her victim with the first blow.

Then it was her complete understanding of this marvel that is the Human male. She understood their infallible index. That gave her a GPS kind of understanding of the character of the person. Once that was achieved she knew how to play her game. From there on this play was a one sided, outcome concluded game.

In her analysis of Aniruddh she gathered he was sexually starved. Maybe his sexual appetite was not being catered to by his wife, she wasn't exactly sure. But she knew that he was fishing for something more. Just the fact that Aniruddh didn't have the guts to move in with the many women he was dilly dallying with. She decided that he needed to be satiated. She decided to let him be completely besotted by her. That way the others would be no competition. When he got everything that he sought in a woman from her, why would he look elsewhere was her reasoning.

She decided to 'chat' with him because for him that was an easy mode of communication. He'd make his move in seemingly innocuous and innocent overtures. Just when that 'oh you are so naughty' element was visible by the other person, he'd make his opening gambit. Most times it was only textual flirtations, some sexting but very few times had these fruition into a full-blown physical, illicit, dangerous sexual encounter.

First it began with official stuff. Then it took a turn to a 'what are you doing now'? She sent him that first entrance statement of hers.

"I was just thinking of you."

"Really? What were you thinking about." That was his usual response.

Now they'd begun fencing with each other. Both knew the next move. It was a game of guessing who'd make that first move. It was a play.

"Just wondering whether what you do at home. Are you working? Are you with your family?" She asked.

"Nah, family is just a drama. Arranged marriage, then kids and what not. There was no fizz in the marriage from day one. There was no open communication. We are two souls living together under the same roof." He would say like the martyr that he wanted to portray himself.

That would give the other person, in this case Helen, a hint that he was not very happy in his marriage. Most times the 'target' would also be someone almost always in the same way – bored relationship, nothing going and as Aniruddh said – no fizz.

"So, I just come home, make pleasant conversations with everyone, go to my space and then 'work' on stuff and then make more meaningless small talk and then perhaps have dinner and hit the sack." He said.

Now was the time to insert a message. "I was just getting ready to go to bed. Showered, changed, spent time with my mother had dinner." She just let that hang in there.

Helen in the shower. Aniruddh's blood pressure just skyrocketed.

"What do you wear when you go to bed usually? I don't wear pyjamas. I just wear a pair of Bermuda shorts and a comfortable t-shirt." He said.

"I too wear just that." She said.

"Nothing else inside." He blurted suddenly not able to keep it within himself.

Pat came the coy answer. "Naughty boy." She almost whispered that into the phone with tantalizing effect.

"Wish I was there." He said.

"Why what would you do here?" She asked, Innocence personified.

"Kiss you deep". He said barely able to speak. He needed to drink some water. His throat was parched.

"Ohhh," She whispered back conspiratorially.

"What are you wearing inside your t-shirt?" He asked, almost frantic to get her clothes off in his mind.

There was a pause. A deliberate pregnant with imagination pause.

"Hello? Helen?" Aniruddh asked wondering if she'd cut the phone.

"Nothing." She was still whispering.

"Oh my God." He said. "I really wish I was there." He repeated.

"Why? What would you do?" She teased openly.

"I would have eaten you." Now the gloves were off. He was getting bolder.

"Oh, you're now getting very naughty." She teased him.

There was this pregnant silence. She knew where she would go with this. But he was tentative. Not sure. He wanted some assurance.

she sent him a heart emoji.

"I would take your face in my hands, cup it gently. Kiss you all over." He said amorously.

"Oh!" She almost gasped in feigned delight.

"What happened to you suddenly?" She asked.

"I have fallen in love with you from the moment I set my eyes on you." He said in that drunken with love state.

"Are you home alone?" She asked him.

"No, everyone is on their own trip. We rarely talk. She does her thing. I am doing my stuff. We have our spaces well defined. We live under the same roof, but we are not very close." He explained.

All the men in her life with whom she had affairs had told her exactly the same story. Of course she knew they were lying. But she didn't give them a clue that she knew. She just kept them imagining that they had fooled her and they had gotten her to believe that they were in love with her – and there were those who had fallen in love with her, though.

By the time Aniruddh Pant came into her life she was a skilled manipulator, a woman who knew her mark like the back of her hand.

"Please be careful." She advised him.

"Yes, of course." He said almost immediately. This one line assured the men that she was okay to go along with whatever they had in mind provided they were careful not to get caught with their spouses.

"Mwah." He typed on his phone.

"I feel shy." She said.

"I want you to know that I am quite open minded and that I am not the usual male macho who just goes wham bam thank you ma'am. I am gentle and considerate. You are a human being. You too have feelings. So you can express your feelings with me openly." He said to her encouraging her to be her expressive best.

"But I am not experienced or anything like that." She said quietly.

"What do you feel like doing now?" He asked her.

"I am scared. Shy. I try to hide my fear and my shyness by being bold when I dress. So that people don't think I am weak and pry upon me." She told him softly.

The trap was laid out. Damsel in distress. In rides the macho. And he rode in like the fool high on sex and pumping sexual curiosity adrenalin. It was also a thrill. He was texting her from within touching distance of his wife. There's that inner thought within him – Wow! What a dude I am. Here with my wife and mentally with someone else.

"You can trust me. What do you feel like doing now." He persisted.

From the time she became pubescent, the one thing that she had drilled into her head was Trust No Man. The second thing that Life taught her as she grew older was – Trust no Man.

Once a long time ago she wanted to pick up a bar of chocolate for herself from the local store she'd learnt that age was no bar for a wicked-minded man.

The middle-aged man behind the counter eyed her walking in. Growing up in an area like Bandra in Bombay, being Catholic – she was not tied down by a dress code that was mandatory for her friends from other walks of life. But being well endowed was also a problem. And she was not averse to pocketing a few things she took a fancy to that her pocket money wouldn't support purchase of. You could call it shoplifting? But to her – it wasn't a sin. Perhaps store inventory was discovered missing after she'd made a raid but wasn't caught? She wouldn't know. Helen could tell what people were thinking by the way they looked at her. These are basic survival skills on the street.

Her favourite eat was a bar of chocolate to be consumed all by herself. That lusciousness captivated her taste buds even before the chocolate hit it. When that taste hit her memory, she would salivate! That was Chocolate's Power over her. And she knew only one brand – Cadbury's. Nothing else was available. So whatever was available and considered best – was the best.

The fact that she'd not have the money to buy a bar all the time didn't bother her. She'd buy it if she could. Else she'd just lift it. Hiding it on her person was easy. But getting to a spot in the small shop where she'd be away from the gaze of those eyes at the cash counter.

Once she had what she wanted, she'd almost waltz her way to the cash counter, pull down her t shirt or dress so that her cleavage was exposed. She knew the smile to wear that would wean those eyes away from her hands to where she wanted them to look. Once they did, the mouth would turn into a lascivious smile.

Once or twice he tried to touch her and she stepped back. When those eyes pleaded, she signalled money with her fingers and she gave him a twenty. She didn't even touch it. She teased him more and then his greasy fingers dipped into the till and came up with a hundred. That was more money than most people earned in her neighbourhood in an hour of actual working.

By now when someone told her that she was to trust them – this was a signal. Talk to me and I am willing to open my wallet, amongst other things.

She wanted this man wrapped round her little fingers and she knew that the longer she delayed the 'show' the more he'd be willing to give.

"Are you busy?" He pinged her.

"No, I was just thinking." She said.

"About what?" He persisted.

He was so horny now that all he could think of was undressing her. Nothing else. And somewhere in his psyche he had gotten past her 'defence', her 'no's. From here on it was a home run.

"I was just thinking that it could be dangerous for you to be texting me from home. We could speak when you are alone." She texted almost conspiratorially.

"That's great. We will meet privately." He texted back.

"In the meantime, read something that I wrote while you were silent. I was thinking about you, how we would interact with each other when we met. You tell me what you think about that. It just came to me in a flash of the mind." He texted.

"What did you write." She wrote.

"Softly playing music

On the radio

A love story

Humming the tune

Sashaying across him

Her smile radiating

Amorously to him -

Throws a kiss

Her beloved soulmate

Aquamarine blue silk

Sheathed this nymphet

In breathtaking voluptuousness

He breathed in

Her fragrant aroma

Came up to him

Wine to drink

On the couch

Laid her soulmate

Warm lips parted

Moist desire tasted

Tongues on fire

Mingled as one.

" There's more, he literally gasped. But that is for later." He texted her.

"Where did you get it from" She texted back, reading it quickly.

"I wrote this for you." He texted back.

Her silence was maddening. He was very nearly tempted to just call her. But then – his whole family was sitting in front of him!

"I have no words." She nailed him to her Cross. Without saying so she told him succinctly that she accepted his advances.

"We will talk later." He texted back.

"Looking forward." She texted.

Post that there had been several long drives, clandestine meetings and even a hotel stay. He bought her gifts, exchanged his notes at work and told her just about everything she wanted to know. In return she gave of herself to him , satiated him to the point of slavery. She got him to the extent that he'd do anything for her.

For Aniruddh – it was exactly the opposite. He thought that he had working for him one of the finest minds that he could ever appoint as an assistant, who was working for him, under him and madly in love with him.

He'd have been extremely shocked to find out the truth.

❑❑❑

Chapter 5: The Investigation

When Pratap Rao Singh walked into the scene of the crime he came in with the notion that it was destiny that brought him there. Otherwise, he asked himself, how could someone from so far away – geographically speaking – be in a place so far removed from his roots, from his usual beat be brought to a place like this?

He shook his head almost in acknowledgement – Yes, Destiny it is. He almost muttered to himself.

The constable standing next to him immediately heard the comment and said, "Sir what is destiny?"

Without missing a beat Pratap Rao Singh said in his usual nonchalant manner, "That you are born to decent hard working parents who had no inkling that despite that best prayers they would bring forth a donkey like you into this world."

Have you seen that slow motion turn of the head when someone says something incredulous? Jaw open? Eyes wide open in utter shock? With that silent speech uttering, "What did you just say?" But you can't say anything just then because s/he happens to be your boss or your superior or even your parent?

That was exactly how the constable looked. Except in his silent response he did say, "Behn***, one day I will become inspector and you will come across me and I will tell you something better."

"Don't say anything because it is your bad karma that brought you here to work for me. So complete your karma without any more obligations towards me." Pratap Rao Singh said almost as if he had read the man's mind.

Psychology does help. Pratap Rao Singh muttered to himself again.

This time, perhaps because the constable was still stewing in the previous comment, he didn't say anything but just kept clenching his jaws almost as if his teeth were threatening to jump out of his mouth.

Pratap Rao Singh always wanted to be in august company. Especially after he became a Police Officer. There was this unwritten rule in the police force. You may not become IPS. You may not even make it to an officer rank. But work under an IPS or a state cadre officer. Make yourself valuable. That officer will remember you wherever s/he goes. And the chances that you will get to work in their periphery is quite high.

There were two ways of doing that. Kiss ass or do diligent work.

Pratap Rao Singh didn't like kissing ass. He was over-educated for his post. He was quite intelligent and he considered that he was smarter than most of the criminals that he'd met so far. Somewhere in his journey to his current posting he'd learnt a little bit of diplomacy.

And therefore he appraised his boss Mr. Malik, the DGP about the case and that he was handling it.

He didn't suffer fools lightly. This constable was that kind that came into the force with one quality. They left their spine in their hometowns. So they'd bend supine in front of any star studded shoulder. They'd do the most menial of tasks. It was almost as if they'd resigned themselves to the category of people that were called The Brainless.

He had to call the SP in the evening to brief him about the subject. So far all he had got was theories. Gossip. Trash that was not even fit for the worst yellow tabloids. He needed something better. A possible motive. A possible suspect. Modus Operandi.

He knew that one of the possibilities of such an outcome was with the General Manager Aniruddh.

Pratap Rao Singh had a methodology before meeting with suspects. First was – Go with an open mind. Second, assess the suspect quickly by ascertaining his background, his personal motive, other angles and then move in for the kill. He was a Sigmund Freud buff to the core. Pratap Rao Singh believes Sigmund Freud to have said that a man likes or dislikes another man or for that matter woman within 7 seconds. Whether Freud said that or not he didn't know for sure but in his own life he'd known that to be a fact. Travelling in a train, it took seven seconds for him to decide whether or not to indulge in a conversation with a fellow passenger. Sometimes he did. Sometimes he did not. When he did the conversation lasted all the way to their destination and in some cases they were friends beyond the journey.

Therefore Pratap Rao Singh believed – especially since he was also a Psychologist – that he'd be able to 'read' a suspect even before an interrogation began.

When Aniruddh appeared before Pratap Rao Singh it was a very frightened-of-the-ensuing-consequences man who knew nothing of Police interrogation techniques, but had heard a lot of unthinkable horror stories in the lock up. When faced with a personality such as Pratap Rao Singh, Aniruddh shrank in his own self esteem. The way the Police Inspector looked at him made him look like he was already convicted of the crime.

Before there was any formal introductions as he imagined would happen – Pratap Rao Singh immediately said, " Just tell me exactly what happened here and I will save you the trip to the police station. What happens here and what happens there, the manner in which we speak, the manner in which I ask you will differ. I don't care for your rank, your degree or your social status. I will treat you with the same indifference I treat every criminal I confront."

This was the classic cop take down. Bring down the suspect to his knees before it even began. Take away the masks.

The position in society. The education. The who-I-am – everything. Inside the police station they even strip you down to your underclothes. It's nothing but to strip you of the last vestige of your self-respect. When that is also stripped, you cease to exist as you did on the outside. You beg. For decency. For a glass of water. To use the loo. They bring you down to your vulnerable best. Then they move in for the kill. A little rough handed treatment if that is needed. A veiled threat works at times. Sometimes not. Your lawyer comes in after all that 'welcome to the police station' is over and done with. By which time you either say yes to whatever you are charged with or you just want to get out.

Most people say that they are not the same person that went in through a police enquiry after they come out. That is if they come out. If they graduate to the prison system, well that's another metamorphosis. The prison system was, ironically designed to re-adjust a human being unfit of being in a normal society. Realignment. But that rarely happens in any prison of the world. When you go in you go in innocent. Regardless of whatever you are charged with. When you come out, you are part of a brotherhood. Society is your enemy. The police aren't trust worthy. Everyone is out to get your back. There are few examples of people who have come out of the prison system who have been transformed.

Aniruddh had heard all this before. But he'd never imagined that he'd be in a position one day to be in that very same spot in his lifetime.

His marriage would be the first casualty. His wife would leave him now for sure. Earlier when they had quarrels and their frequent spats would turn ugly – she threatened him with divorce. But she didn't have anywhere to go to. Common sense prevailed. Better the devil rather than the deep sea. Or he'd imagine – society needs to see a happily married couple. So play the role. Appear in a few parties holding hands and looking at other people. Smiling empty smiles in front of nameless people smiling equally empty smiles. Pretending to be friends for ever and bitch the moment their backs are turned. That was the formula. Therefore play it.

Both were in their safe zones. She was still a faithful wife. He was not. He had Helen. But he was not averse to a quick one night stands.

His career with this company would end.

His kids would detest him.

What was he left with?

His animal instincts kicked in. He decided to befriend the Inspector and 'take him into his confidence' – almost like saying I will help you crack this case. But keep me out of it deal. He didn't know if the Inspector would take the bait.

But then Aniruddh had learnt from his Boss the Founder of the company in which he worked who'd often say – Pull the Mountain with a Strand of your hair. You get it you get a mountain. You don't, so what? You just lost a strand of your hair. You got lots more! No harm trying.

And so his demeanour quickly changed when he'd arrived at this strategy point in his mind. It is strange, how when you decide what to do, half the demons of fear that you created in your head disappear almost magically.

"Sure Inspector, I will be as helpful as I possibly can. But before we begin, may I introduce myself properly." Aniruddh said.

Within a few seconds the Inspector was receiving his business card and although the Inspector wasn't carrying his own, he sufficed it with a 'you know who I am.'

"May I offer you some breakfast? You and your men? I see you have been here for a while, but I am not sure if you have been looked after." He asked the Inspector.

"Well we are not here to party. But having said that I think I will have some breakfast." The Inspector said.

Aniruddh believed that he had won a point here. Now they were two human beings caught up in a terrible situation. From here on it was who would get the better hand over the other.

While breakfast was being summoned, Aniruddh briefly told the Inspector about what had happened, why they were all gathered here in the resort and what was the agenda and the entire rigmarole.

Without even being asked about his clandestine relationship with Helen he told the Inspector that he was having a relationship with her.

He put that down to proximity at work, similar problems, long hours spent in each other's company, being able to communicate freely and openly about each other's problems without the 'judgemental' angle which happens when you discuss the same issues with a spouse, or a best friend.

However, he assured the Inspector, there was no love or anything like that. This was mere lust. This was an expression at its most naked best.

"I really don't know who'd have done this to her." He anguished, finally wringing his hands together in palpable distress.

Inspector Pratap Rao Singh had polished off his breakfast and was on his second cup of sugary tea when Aniruddh finished his tale of heartbreak.

He didn't say anything except look at Aniruddh during his narration briefly, taking his eyes off his breakfast filled plate.

Finally he said, "Well I heard you. But I am not the Judge, the jury or the executioner. As Investigating Officer I have to tell you that I have reason to believe that you have motive to kill and therefore I hold you as a prime suspect. Whatever you just said will be used against you in a court of law even though I should have said that before you began your little speech. Since you are a responsible member of this organization, I am not arresting you just yet. But I want you to give me your wife's mobile number and your boss's mobile number so that I can contact them just in case you decide to 'disappear'. I hope you understand – I am letting you walk out of here not because I accept your 'stress buster relationship theory'. I know you have a family and that you are a senior member of this management and I think you should maintain the status quo till something changes. Till then you are not to leave my jurisdiction and you should be available to take my calls at all times. I will not have you message me "I will call you later. I am in a meeting." Whatever time, whatever the place you are in – you will take my calls, as and when I call you. Is that clear?" Inspector Pratap Rao Singh asked.

Aniruddh realized that his strategy had only worked for some time. But he was grateful that he was not being arrested on suspicion and that he could go home from here.

Suddenly Pratap turned behind and asked ' Are you the one responsible for Helen's suspected pregnancy?'

'No..' Anirudh's eyes remained unpleasantly wide and left the meeting.

Inspector Pratap Rao Singh took out his notebook and began to draw a column. Name – Number – Relationship to Victim.

This is how it looked like.

Name	Number	Position in Co	Relationship to Victim	Priority of Suspicion	Date of Entry	Motive
Aniruddh	99234*****	GM	Clandestine Lover and Reporting Manager	#1	Today	Suppress an Illicit affair
Pandey	99234*****	PA / Peon / Eyes and Ears		Not now	Today	Has no motive

He called Pandey on his cell phone. It had barely rang once before Pandey ji answered.

"Hukum Sarkar." He whispered on the phone.

"Aur baaki logon ko bhejo. Mere paas bahut time nahin hai idhar" He spoke brusquely on the phone.

"Sir I will send you Jeeva sir, our Sales Manager." Pandey Ji said. It was like he'd decided whom to send and when to the Inspector. After all this was power, isn't it, he said to himself. Even the police needed his help to meander through this company's politics!

❑❑❑

Chapter 6: Jeeva Rao

Having spent the better part of his younger years in devoting time to a career, Jeeva Rao had decided a few years ago that he would retire in the company that he'd first joined.

Too much time had gone by for him to now look for another opportunity in another organization. As a Sales Manager, relationships had been made with customers. Relationships that had now progressed into friendships. Trust had been developed. In some cases, these relationships were like old family bonds.

His relationship with the owners of the company had also matured over the years. There is the time in the life of an employee when a senior or a boss has to handhold him or her. Be taught the subtle nuances of a job. Then there is a time when there is an opportunity to fly solo in the job almost without supervision.

Born into a family of old-world traditions and beliefs, Jeeva Rao had completed his schooling and college in educational institutions where the middle-class throng. There was nothing to do but study. There was no sports. No other intellectual activities like debating or participating in quizzes or competing in such activities with other schools. Here was an almost factory-like environment where you come to study, excel in it or just complete your education.

In a city like Bombay there were many schools like this. South Indians were thronging into the city looking for clerical jobs in the many textile mills that dotted the city. So it was not surprising that Jeeva's father found himself a job as a stenographer in one of the city's leading mills near Dadar. Matunga was where the South Indians thronged to and it was not long before the area became a Mecca for South Indians to congregate, to discuss matters from back home. It was here that even marriages happened. Almost as if the South Indian diaspora in Mumbai had decided that they'd make this city their home.

And home it was for the many who came here from South India. To prop up the demand for education of their wards, schools sprouted. Slowly they grew into colleges. Even their favourite Carnatic Music was taught and it was not long before the now famous Shanmukhananda Hall came up. Eminent artists – particularly from the South – came to perform. It soon became a cultural hub. Such was its prominence that being on the Executive Panel of the Managing Committee was like a revered social status.

Growing up in these parts was like the shaping of a mind in multiple disciplines. The local language was Marathi of course. Hindi used a stop gap arrangement. Most South

Indians could only speak a stammering Hindi. Some did better as they were taught Hindi in their own schools back home as a second language.

English was the medium of instruction in the local schools that the children of the South Indian 'immigrants' went to. The more affluent of them were sent to the schools that were run by the Christian Church – the convents.

Therefore these kids grew up being multilingual. They were exposed to different cultures and in the same colony where a typical South Indian family resided you'd often find local Maharashtrians, a smattering of Catholics and in those days maybe a family or two of Muslims.

Depending on where you lived your language skills were accordingly shaped. Jeeva found himself living inside the Mill Quarters and there was a far more ethnic mix than perhaps Matunga.

By the time he graduated he was fluent in three or four languages including Marathi. His Marathi was so good that many a time he passed off as a Maharashtrian. Bombay itself had metamorphosed into a new name. She was re-christened. Mumbai was born. Just like the city, it took that much of an evolution to become a Mumbaikar and after a generation or two that is what these citizens became. No more South Indian or North Indian – though they retained much of their hierarchical traditions, their cooking and their core essence – they had become more than just a labelled group of people.

A Mumbaikar was versatile, worldly wise, resilient – amongst other things. S/he was stoic about the many challenges that the city threw up her citizens from time to time. There was a saying that if you could live in Mumbai you could live anywhere in the world.

College came and went quickly for Jeeva. The day was full for a young college going kid in Mumbai. There was the necessary commute. Then a whole day of either attending college or pretending to – and then there was friends and all that other thing about growing up in an adolescence innocence with young girls and all that. It was difficult to be sane all the time and the insanity did rear its head sometimes. A smoke was offered. Your head screams that you should decline but your hand reaches out for it. The peer pressure is easier to handle than the angry denial of the parents who'd 'sacrificed so much' to ensure that a decent education was made possible! Sometimes a glass of beer was offered, a cold glass of beer that pushed aside the sultry weather for a moment.

But to a large extent he stayed out of harm's way and graduated with top marks much to the admiration of his parents and his entire colony.

Getting a job was another whole different challenge and it was not easy to come by one. The Times of India "Opportunities" section was a necessary and literal 'dive into' for job seekers and post that there would be several marked circles of job announcements that showed some promise.

That was how he'd come up with this job. Sales Executive for Maharashtra region. He ticked the first few 'must have skills' for the job. Marathi speaker, manage Hindi, communicate well in English, pleasing personality – that was a must for a Sales Exec those days – Male only – that was also quite openly mentioned and easiest one was – high level of integrity. Somewhere at the end of the ad was mentioned – a graduation in any discipline was compulsory!

He presented himself well on the day of the interview at a local hotel in Dadar. Starched white shirt, a borrowed time that sat awkwardly on his throat in a knot that was too big but then there was no arguing with D'Costa uncle who was the local expert in suits and ties and all that - having married off three daughters in the best possible weddings that the entire colony had ever witnessed!

When his turn came one of the interviewers in the panel spoke to him in Marathi and he answered very easily. Perhaps that was the only question that the gentleman was asked to ask because he never spoke after that first opening salvo. Then it was all in English and Hindi – perhaps by the most authoritative person in the interviewing group – the owner of the company.

It was an hour of almost gruelling questions and answers. He was a BCom student – there wasn't much asked about the subject per se. It was all more to do with his own parents, what he'd learnt from his father or his mother that would be his own guiding principles in his life – questions like that. He felt that they were trying to explore whether he'd fit the 'integrity point' and by the time it was over – the Senior told him to wait in the lobby.

After about an hour or more – he couldn't really tell – he was asked to submit his documents and they said that he was selected to join as a Sales Executive.

That was how Jeeva Rao entered into the employ of this organization where he was for almost 20 odd years. He'd seen many upheavals. He faced many challenges. But his work was exemplary. He found that in sales relationships mattered the most. The sale happened next. If you could develop relationships then your sales didn't matter. He was an expert at relationship building and slowly but surely Jeeva took the sales of the company into digits that they'd never experienced.

The management was shrewd. They knew a performer when they saw one and they did not hesitate to reward him. First it was larger territories and then it was positional hikes and just like that he'd made it into a Management cadre.

Somewhere along the way a young MBA Graduate had joined the company. He was from a premier institute and he'd impressed the owners and the management at the time that he'd do a great job. So they hired him. Aniruddha Pant made his grand entry and to say that he was not a cultural fit was an understatement. From an Upper Middle Class family background, boasting a finesse and a social upbringing that almost seemed like a boast factor to the others in the organization – Aniruddha was not a great hit. But he was hard working, he was amiable in his disposition and he was careful not to make enemies. But his hire seemed to send a message to the existing team that the Management was not averse to hiring a different breed of employees, going forward.

Just recently they made a decision that didn't go down with many. But by then there were external investors in the company. They wanted to see faster growth. They wanted to waste no time in the slow and laborious processes that were till then employed by the company as its growth tactics. Better Product, better Service, Better technology – those were the new mantra's that was being employed. To deploy these into the market the management felt that they needed more aggressive foot soldiers and that is how Aniruddha was brought in.

Within a few short years it was clear that the management favoured Aniruddha and he was promoted to head the Management team as its General Manager.

A drop of curd can curdle an entire pail of milk – so the saying goes. The daggers were out almost immediately. Jeeva was aiming to be picked for the position because of his knowledge of the dealers and distribution network, his ability to convince them to remain faithful to this brand and for his internal relationship skills. That was just at the top. Even at the bottom of the pyramid the promotion didn't go down very well. A rank outsider came from nowhere and was going to rule over them. It was like a pall of uncertain gloom had overcome the company.

Jeeva and Aniruddha maintained a decent relationship. But Jeeva was not happy deep down in his heart. A resentment began to grow. That became evident in meetings when sales figures were discussed. Aniruddha was towing the Investors line of aggressive growth and the first point of resistance to deploy such a strategy was from Jeeva Rao. He had built up the sales network in a slow and steady manner. Now he was being told to do whatever he'd done faster.

"Relationships cannot be built overnight." Jeeva once countered.

"Arrey, we have a superior product. Our Customer service is fabulous. Plus we a technology which allows both the distribution network and the customer a better access to the product and thereby the company." Aniruddha countered.

Both the men realized that they were not going to kowtow to each other. The lines were drawn. The fight would continue. Till there was nothing to fight about.

Aniruddha was ambitious as hell and he knew what he could achieve if he could implement and bring to fruition the grandiose plans that were drawn up for this company by the investors and the 're-aligned to new purpose' owners and by now almost old management.

For him Jeeva Rao was just another body that he might have to hop over to achieve his own personal dreams in this organization. He was not going to take any prisoner and his body language, his working style was perfectly aligned with the investors idea of how to run an organization.

It is strange how when appointments are made at the top they create walls way down below in an organization. There's nothing physical, there's nothing to even suspect of such divisions – but the walls are tangible. Territories are marked. Venturing into another turf sans an invitation isn't encouraged. Information isn't accessible even if its summoned from "higher ups" – and that is how it was between Jeeva and Aniruddha.

This 'rivalry' soon turned into a deep rooted jealousy. Each man was gunning for the first opportunity to blame the other. Blame games began – subtly at first.

Finally just before a board meeting was due, Jeeva stormed angrily into Aniruddha's cabin and wanted to know why he had altered the sales figures that he'd submitted to the Board.

"I have clearly sent you an email with detailed projections." He said matter of factly.

"Yes. But those numbers are not acceptable to the Management." Aniruddha told him clearly in no uncertain terms.

"They may not be – but that is the reflection of the market factors. I cannot change that. You change the numbers, and it is then my headache to go out and try to achieve those numbers." Jeeva said – almost on the back foot.

"The market is set to grow Jeeva. We want to get to a market leadership position. Your numbers will not assure that prediction. We have to grow faster, and we need to sell better. As General Manager this is my responsibility to achieve, and I will have to do that. Whatever you say is strictly between you and me but that is not the position of the Board and this management." Aniruddha said almost sternly.

Jeeva knew when he was beaten and he simply said, "At this rate, we will lose our dealers and we will lose our current market standings."

"Is that your promise or is that a general statement based on your outdated selling style?" Aniruddha asked him almost in a cynical tone.

"I have built up this network from scratch and I know each and every one of these distributors – our first-line customers. I know how they operate. I know their pulse. You sit here and all you do is to make promises to the Board and the Management that cannot be achieved. When the final count happens and there is a gap between projections and actuals you will quietly blame us all for non-performance. I know you well. I know what you will do. And I will not let that happen." Jeeva told him bluntly.

"You take a call – you can let me know. Whether you want to make this plan that I have submitted happen or not. The point is this Jeeva – Those numbers will be achieved. The only question is – whether it will happen with you or without you. That is your decision. Not mine. I think I have made myself clear. So you please decide and let me know." Aniruddha looked at Jeeva directly and told him off. Then he lowered his gaze to his laptop almost as if to say – This meeting is over.

Non-verbal communication is not taught that much, but it is easily picked up when deployed. Just that look, that body language or even that bang of a cup on the table – is so explosively loud and clear that there is almost zero ambiguity, especially by those who are the targets.

Jeeva turned on his heel and walked out of Aniruddha's cabin.

"I will fix you, Mister. You don't know me. You just awakened your worst nightmare." He muttered ominously under his breath.

A simmering discontent

The Policeman in Pratap Rao Singh was not content with the explanation that was being elicited by his endeavours interviewing the usual suspects.

What was obvious was just two plain facts. Nothing could alter that. There were no two other explanations for that.

One was that there was a dead woman at the scene. Prima Facie it didn't look like a natural death. Although the modus operandi had to be ascertained and the motive for her death had to be investigated.

Second – the killer was not someone who'd escaped from there.

He was there amongst them, thinking that he'd outsmarted everyone. He or she was a dangerous person, beyond the usual flight or fight mental state. In fact – during his several years in the police force he had realized a few things, especially in a murder investigation.

Murder was usually a spur of the moment, in the heat of an argument occurrence or else it was plain old fashioned planned connived murder for whatever pecuniary gain or concealment.

Whenever Inspector Pratap Rao Singh had investigated a crime scene he'd look around at the people gathered. Sometimes that murderer would lurk amongst the spectators and see what the police were learning. Whether they were onto the real architect or the executioner of the crime.

Sometimes his eyes would actually lock into the eyes of the bystanders. In that one instant, a primeval recognition would dawn upon him. That one instant was enough for panic to set into the killer's otherwise cool nonchalant mental ambience. Suddenly for no apparent reason – the person would make a bolt for it. Or do something that would immediately alert the Policeman's bristling instinct.

The Unwitting Suspect usually made an appearance in the case as a casual enquirer, as a friendly and helpful witness or just happened to be around wanting to catch a bit of the 'gossip'.

The straight and proper interrogation wasn't producing the necessary results. He needed to break through with a suspect. He needed to report to his bosses. Then there was his own personal and professional pride. He was assigned this case because this was his turf. That would only cut some ice for a while. Beyond that, the State CID would step in. They were in another league. The file would be transferred with a "No Progress by Local PD, re-assigned to CID" and that is something he did not want.

There is more than one way to investigate a crime. The Sherlock Holmes way of clever thinking and deduction uses a certain sense of craftiness by sending out information to the very crime scene players making them feel that there's a breakthrough in the case.

Pratap Rao Singh also knew another way. Observation. Observe everything carefully and it will reveal to you what you didn't find in the preliminary but hurried search of a crime scene.

Lastly, he was a Psychologist. A person's body language "spoke" to the policeman more than the person would reveal about himself. Eyes spoke even though the tongues remained silent or professed innocence. The voice changed when it was mouthing anything that was far from the truth.

Therefore he knew that that he needed to look around. Get a feel of the people gathered here at this remote venue for this conference.

Just then a sense of resolve hit him and he mouthed the words that seemed to have arrived on some celestial carriage almost like a bolt of lightning that came from beyond.

"I will crack this."

Man endeavours by the fruits of his labour, he'd once read somewhere. But he'd realized in Life that if those efforts were substantiated by the Grace of God – success was a guaranteed result. Otherwise, Man would toil on and on with no end in sight and when the end does present itself, it flees away suddenly almost as if in some sudden fright.

This "Bolt from Beyond" was just what Pratap Rao Singh needed and he was filled with sudden inspiration and new motivation.

As someone who was fond of reading Corporate Drama stories and who'd been privy to Corporate Crimes, he'd seen his share of the Corporate world's not-so-glitzy side and he wanted to explore that side in this current chapter of his investigation.

He realized that the news of the 'unnatural elevation' spread like wildfire within the organization's walls and even beyond the very marketplaces where the organization's revenue was forthcoming.

Helen was closest to the epicentre of the action. She was making out the letters, despatching was handled by Pandey ji. Dissemination of company facts or secrets was not really announced as much as it travelled across the length and breadth by word of mouth. Grapevine. Gossip. Call it whatever you want to. The Inspector was witness to the unwritten powers that someone as low in the organization as Pandey ji warranted.

Those that spread it were either asked to do so because they were in the position to spread the word or whatever they said was immediately believable. Pandey ji because of his proximity to the Senior Management and the Board was, in a manner of speaking, close to the upper echelon but didn't belong to that very class that he catered to. He was uniformed staff, took his meals in the general cafeteria and was careful to mix with the top of the class therein. He would sit with the foremen, the supervisory cadre and the junior office staff. Although they all knew that he was not a chronic gossip monger – the senior foremen and supervisors would get golden snippets of information from him from time to time.

This information leak was often deliberate. It sometimes mitigated the real impact of what was to come. When the effect was conveyed back upstairs the feedback was weighed and carefully analysed. Pay rises were the most common of the Top Secret Info leaks engineered.

The Inspector also realized that there was another factor. It was the promotions.

Aniruddha Pant was a go getter for the Management and Board. But for the people lower down they resented his pushy attitude. They treated that as his characteristic behaviour which it was not. He had a job to do and he was aggressive about achieving that. As he often said to those that didn't like his behaviour – I didn't come here to win your vote of confidence or the Most Friendly Manager – I came here to do a job and I will do just that.

. This is something that was happening right across many legacy companies where they'd grown to their current dispensation. A founder who'd bootstrapped the company and then grew it over a few decades. Thereupon a new set of investors were onboarded, and they'd always come in with a new set of rules that often ran quite the opposite to what was the rote. That set in some anxiety. Heads would roll, old hands would be replaced and without so much of an apparent change – work culture changed ever so subtly.

Relationships, old world bonhomie and an inter-dependability drove many of these businesses to their growth. Combined with masterful Leadership, nothing was Impossible. But when you change the basics of human dynamics there was some hell to pay for. A certain lethargy or I-don't-care syndrome sets in. A distinct lack of ownership is palpable. Why the very energy of a high achieving work place changed. If that was not remedied fast enough then the very business took a hit.

Then – people notice things.

How other people behave with each other. Particularly hierarchical behaviour. More so the exhibited behaviour between male and female colleagues.

A man's very gait changes when he is in the company of a woman whom he is interested in. His smile changes. His voice changes. Overall – his very demeanour changes. It might not be overtly visible to many – but those who observe the small things pick it up instantly.

Aniruddha's post lunch walk with Helen was noticed almost immediately. This was a ritual. People walked a little just after their meal. Especially the managerial class. The factory worker would find a tree or a comfortable bench and stretch out and try to manage a few winks before the bell clanged its get back to work noisy announcement.

There were eyes everywhere and the eyes saw, created content for the tongues to wag and combined with the 'dissent' of the management style, the stories that were set loose were vulgar and salacious.

Inspector Pratap Rao Singh's notes were now talking to him. He summarized in his little note book about who he was after for the murder of Helen apart from the obviously suspicious.

Someone who didn't like what was going on. You wanted to hurt the organization. You didn't want to be caught. With this one act you'd have removed the obvious suspect. Because his entire 'immoral affair' would now lie open and exposed and he'd lose his job, if he was not actually booked for the murder.

Instead of continuing with the usual style of interrogation Inspector Pratap Rao Singh decided to call someone that even Pandey ji didn't think of sending to meet the Inspector.

The Foreman of the Factory – Patwardhan Jamnalal. He was as old as the factory. Came in when the organization was formed. 12th standard of the Original ISC Board. Due to various circumstances couldn't pursue his education and having to look after his family, took the first job that he'd come across. Lab assistant with high school diploma, Science as Major.

He was the typical understudy to a Genius that you'd ever come across. The company hired some of the best chemical brains that money could buy. It was necessary to build that intellectual proficiency in the market. So in that initial pick of best brains, Patwardhan was hired.

To be in such august company was something that he'd always cherished. When his educational journey was interrupted, he had lost hope. Now with this job – it seemed that there was a chance, after all, to redeem his life.

There was nothing else in his life. He simply threw his all into his job. Long hours, uncomplaining behaviour and a very docile character endeared him to his bosses. He was given additional pay and bonuses, and he was included in confidential product meetings that were a cut or two above his pay grade. But by then – Patwardhan had won the trust of his superiors.

His brain was a ticking computer of formulae and a plethora of permutations and combinations that even his bosses didn't come up with. This little man in the R&D lab was a star that they'd stumbled upon and they kept that secret to themselves. Of course, they fed him with bits and pieces of tidbits – salary hikes out of the ordinary, commendation letters, and as time passed by – a small cabin at the end of the lab – much smaller than his bosses but a cabin nevertheless for someone not even in the Management cadre.

As the years passed, people came and went, but Patwardhan stayed on. They even told him that he was one of the pillars of the organization. When fifteen years had passed, they presented him with a sleek Titan Slim watch complete with the Company's logo emblazoned on the dial with the number 15.

When you put something like that in someone's head – a certain sense of warped ownership occurs in that person's head. He thinks exactly that – He's an Owner. He behaves like one. He treats others who don't stand up to his yardstick with a certain disdain.

By the time Aniruddha Pant had become General Manager, Patwardhan was an alternative, unofficial power centre. Except that his fiefdom was the production from where it began in the R&D lab to the time it exited the production line filled in boxes ready for the market.

In that space there was nothing anyone could do to alter the status quo writ that Patwardhan controlled. Everyone knew it. No one complained because there was nothing negative to complain about.

Till now.

He wasn't happy with the way the company was run. He wasn't happy in the manner that someone who came 'yesterday' – here he meant both Helen and Aniruddha – could sully the reputation of the organization that he'd helped build over these many years.

For Inspector Pratap Rao Singh that was motive enough.

He added Patwardhan's name to the list that he'd been creating.

Tonight, he'd sit with this Old Monk Rum, Tandoori Chicken, 3 cigarettes, salted peanuts and write the Situation Report to his immediate boss, the ACP (Additional Commissioner of Police). The gist of it would be to tell his Boss that he had a grip on the situation and that his investigation was gaining credence.

❑❑❑

Chapter 7: Shyam Maheshwari

Shyam Maheshwari, the Purchase Manager, sat at his desk, scrolling through his phone with a mixture of boredom and longing. His eyes lingered on the photos of women, his mind wandering to fantasies he dare not acknowledge in his waking life. The facade of a happily married man with three children was a heavy burden to carry, but it had its benefits - job security, social respectability, and a sense of stability. But the real Shyam, the one he hid from the world, was a lustful man who craved excitement and adventure.

At home, Shyam's life was a monotony of routine. His wife, Swati, was a controlling presence, always questioning his whereabouts, his phone bills, and his late nights at work. His children, two sons and a daughter, were demanding and loud, leaving him exhausted by the end of the day. The only solace he found was in his secret online life, where he could escape the drudgery of his domestic existence.

But even that escape was fraught with danger. Swati had installed monitoring software on their home computer, tracking his every click and keystroke. Or so he thought. Shyam had to be careful, always covering his tracks, deleting his browsing history, and using incognito modes. The thrill of the secrecy was exhilarating, but the fear of discovery was always lurking. This double-edged life – a very typical Dr. Jekyl and Mr. Hyde kind of life.

As he worked, his eyes would often drift to the clock, counting down the minutes until he could leave for the day. Not that he looked forward to going home, but at least at work, he had some semblance of control over his life. His team respected him, his bosses appreciated him, and he could lose himself in the mundane tasks of procurement and supply chain management.

But even at work, Shyam couldn't entirely be himself. His computer was a minefield of hidden tabs and secret browsing histories, evidence of his true nature that he dare not let his colleagues discover. The rumours of his indiscretions had already spread, whispers of a crashed computer and telltale signs of his online activities. Shyam had brushed it off as mere gossip, but the fear of being discovered lingered.

And yet, it was Shyam who had been the first to declare Helen's death, his voice trembling with a mix of shock and excitement. He had always lusted after her, but that was a secret he kept hidden, even from his closest colleagues. Now, with her gone, Shyam felt a pang of regret, a sense of opportunity lost.

As the investigation continued, Shyam watched with interest, his mind racing with possibilities. Had he been too obvious in his admiration for Helen? Had someone discovered his secret and taken matters into their own hands? The thought sent a shiver down his spine, and Shyam pushed it aside, focusing on the task at hand - managing the supply chain, and keeping his secrets hidden.

His bosses tolerated him because he was a good bargainer when it came to purchasing stock for the organization. This was one of the biggest expenses on the balance sheet and it was also fraught with corruption. Suppliers were keen on associating with Shyam's organization because they were prompt paymasters. They asked for a hard bargain alright, but payment was never delayed. In his own warped sense, he never accepted any bribes from suppliers! Although that extra income would have augmented his never ending sexual arousal. Funnily enough – this sexual energy would go damp when he was in the presence of his wife. With her his sexual life was almost non-existent. It did cross his mind that she was frustrated because of the fact that she was discontent. Swati was as human as any other person and she did have her own wants and needs. She did her bit to evoke his sexual interest in her by acquiring a whole slew of lingerie which she'd display to him in the dark privacy of their bedroom.

While he would be aroused for a while with her seductive appearance, his mind would not go beyond into participating further.

"What's this, you seem to be growing younger by the day?" He would appear aghast almost as if she'd demanded something that was totally not expected from her.

"Why? Am I a grandmother?" She asked, still not on par with this rejection.

"No, not a grandmother, but we have grown up children and our minds are different now. We are more friends now than lovers. We have to behave according to the times we live in, according to the roles life has attributed upon us." He'd try to squeal.

To play this side, there was this pooja exercise that would go on every morning. Just after he got back from his morning walk, he'd go into the toilet – along with his phone – if possible log onto some xxx site and then masturbate, after which he'd feel really like the day belonged to him. His bath was meticulous – every single part of his body received utmost attention.

Post that came his 3 P's. Powder. Perfume. Parting. He still had the need to use copious volumes of fragrant Ponds Dream Flower Talcum Powder over his body, in his arm pits and between his legs. Then came the head. He still had a good amount of hair and that he oiled well and then using a plastic comb, he'd get that parting right. Full of concentration, his tongue would stick out, his eyes narrowed lest one strand of hair would fall out of place – and then when he was utterly satisfied, he whacked the comb on his towel covered thighs and place it back carefully into its holder on the dressing table.

He wasn't yet ready. Just after that 'dressing up' he'd take out his Pooja Dhoti – which was his attire to present himself before his favorite deity in the small but crowded pooja which his interior decorator had insisted be part of the kitchen but yet amalgamated with the rest of the kitchen décor so that it'd not stand out. So a corner of the pretty large kitchen was the designated area for the pooja and he laid out his mat and sat down cross legged to begin his daily worship.

Lighting the lamp, chanting some ancient mantra and performing the ritual – Shyam Maheshwari was Holiness Personified. Then when the chanting and the offering of the incense sticks were all done, a little bit of prasad was always offered to the Gods. Today it was sticky rice in condensed milk – a fast-food version of the desi kheer – but then – that was not important. What was important was that an offering was being made and the God's would be happy. This was then given to everyone in the house and breakfast would be served only after this elaborate pooja was done!

Then he'd go back into his bedroom to change. What came out of the bedroom was the official Shyam Maheshwari, the veritable purchase manager and with powers and trust way beyond any ordinary purchase manager.

Breakfast at home was a quiet affair. A maid served them all. She just dumped on all their plates what was prepared by the other maid – a cook really – and between the two of them they'd prep the breakfast and lunch tiffin for Shyam and the kids, prepare breakfast and serve it for them. Breakfast was a silent meal – not the that the other meals were full of laughter and talk – but this was a silent meal. Everyone was busy with whatever they chose to be busy with.

The kids wouldn't speak much in front of their parents except if it meant they wanted their attention. Today, there was nothing – so they were silent. Shyam was already onto his phone and his wife was scrolling her Insta reels.

No one in their wildest imagination would ever think that there was anything wrong with this picture-perfect family.

Least of all – no one would ever say that Shyam Maheshwari was lustful, most of his day was occupied with nothing but one thought – sex. His work was almost automated and carried out by a well-orchestrated team. There was nothing rocket science about his purchase department and there was a predictability about its functioning.

When Helen arrived in the company, he immediately made every effort to befriend her. Of course she would talk to everyone. That was Helen. That was what was most endearing about her. She even thanked the office peon when he fetched her a glass of water. But his lust for her overcame everything else.

Suddenly he switched off from his online jaunts. Here was everything that he lusted in a woman. A good physique, a good personality, smart, when she strode into the Management section of the office, she oozed sexuality – the kind of sexuality that turned on his entirety. Then there was this fragrance about Helen, it wafted like a cloud after her presence was long gone. He'd trail it with his nose in the air, enjoying it almost like some animalistic invitation that she'd sprayed for his attention.

He'd tried his best to be 'extra friendly' with Helen. But Helen could be very firm. When she said no, she meant no. So his advances with a hidden agenda were spotted two moments before they were uttered – what came out of his mouth was a lame duck invitation with no zest or anything else close to it.

"One of these day's lets go to that Dhaba on the highway. They say the food is lovely. There are also a couple of spots on the highway which is quite picturesque." He'd suggested.

"Nah, thank you – but Nah. It's too far away and I cannot take time off from home on the weekends because there's tons to do at home, my mother is with me, and I do need to give her time." Helen said, flatly refusing the invitation.

But Shyam Maheshwari was one of those people who believed in the old adage – that if you don't succeed at first, then try and try again. He never gave up easily on his amorous pursuits. He'd flirt at first, if that worked it worked. If that didn't work he was not averse to spending some money. If nothing worked, then he'd have his trusted fist to satisfy his urges!

What really got his goat was when Aniruddha Pant was appointed General Manager – the highest level in Management in this company that an employee could get to. Compounded with that – horror of horrors – Helen was assigned Executive Assistant to Aniruddha Pant. What irked him on a daily basis was seeing them both together, almost as if they were lovers – strutting around after lunch.

"Bitch, she refused to come for a drive with me. Now she's virtually being transported daily from her home by this fellow." He silently tormented.

From then on Shyam Maheshwari's character took on another avatar. That of the spurned lover. That of the jealousy ridden lustful man. In a couple of meetings with the management – he'd pointed out lapses in communication indirectly blaming Helen for not forwarding important files to him. That didn't really work out because Aniruddha handled that beautifully. He thought that Shyam was accusing him and didn't see the hidden intent to take down Helen's efficiency in public. In his defence he inadvertently defended his team which obviously included Helen and that was that.

Now there were two enemies. One was Helen. She whom he dreamt of. She who made him so hard that even he was surprised at his own masculinity. Couple of times he got up from his perch on the living room recliner to go to the bathroom to check his throbbing pencil. He hadn't done anything. Just thought of Helen and he was up! If his wife saw it just now, she'd also not believe that the silent pencil had suddenly got its erect avatar back again! He smiled at his own reflection in the bathroom mirror. One of these days, he promised himself, he'd spend an entire afternoon with his wife. Only thing is that he'd have a couple of drinks and then imagine that it was Helen under him and 'perform'.

The other enemy was Aniruddha Pant who usurped what would have been his. Everything from thereon that Aniruddha did was unacceptable, under par and not becoming of a respectable General Manager.

When his next opportunity with the owners happened, he very humbly submitted his thoughts about the 'current management' to the owners. They listened. They didn't care too much about office politics. That existed even when they ran the organization. What they were interested in was profits. If that was coming in regularly and projections were getting better quarter to quarter, they didn't care too much about anything else. Plus – They didn't need to sweat it out everyday in the factory cum office anymore!

Gossiping is like farming in a manner of speaking. One had to let the information settle in, then when the opportune moment came – a subtle reminder was needed and boom – desired results were harvested. Character assassination, demotions, salary deferral's – whatever punishment needed to be meted out could be done so with great ease. There were people in management who were as pliable as children's clay. Just that one needs to know how to mould it effectively to wreak havoc!

When a few months passed and nothing happened in response to his 'informing the owners' – Shyam Maheshwari decided to take matters into his own hands. He would come up with some plan to defame Aniruddha Pant and then quietly move him out of the organization. Then he'd represent himself as a potential and proven trustworthy candidate for the position and then he'd have Helen. Now she'd have no other way but to acquiesce to his advances.

He almost jumped in glee at the thought and literally patted himself on his brilliant mind.

Chapter 8: Rohit Das Gupta

Son of the infamous rabble-rousing Union Leader, firebrand mass hysteria-causing speaker and sitting MLA for the past four terms Shubodh Das Gupta, Rohit was indeed born with the proverbial silver spoon in his mouth.

His mother was a Union Worker and began an illicit affair with his father during both their hey days. Between gruelling strikes and backdoor negotiations with the management, when the eyes became lustful and even a very touch between his parents would spark an orgasmic outpouring, Rohit Das Gupta was born. On one rainy, humid night in a small dingy little "private" clinic of a midwife he came into the world - a scrawny looking child much unlike his firebrand father or care a damn attitude mother.

A spoilt brat is created, not born was how Father Regi Mathew put it when Rohit was put under the care of the Jesuit convent-run school which also had a boarding facility. Although it was a tightly run ship high on discipline and a good quality of Education, it was back in the day a young institution, with big plans and not much of a budget.

So the money came in the form of donations from rich patrons and parents, parents who wanted the Jesuits to take care of their wards, while they went out and created more wealth and enjoyed the fruits of that wealth without the trouble of having to parent their 'inconvenient children'.

That was how it was – almost from the time he was an infant till about the time he finished high school – Father Regi Mathew was about the closest to a father that Rohit had, something that he would admit to only his own conscience and in some deep drunkenness or drug induced 'another worldness'. Every year there was the 'annual pilgrimage' like vacation to see his by now married parents – but there was a catch. His mother was the 'official second wife' and his father would only come to spend time with him in bits and pieces. Between them there was just a DNA bond and nothing even akin to a father son relationship. With his mother there was a lot of love and affection and she doted every moment he spent with her, Her kindness would rub off on Rohit in a kind of a warped way into his psyche many years later.

Human Beings crave attention and as young children and growing up into adulthood years – we all seek attention. When we don't get it we create situations which makes us the focus of such attention. Some of it is directed – a student studies well and gets good grades and is 'celebrated' as a 'good student' – even there, there are classifications. Some do things which cause trouble not only to the person creating the scenario but also to others – in Rohit's case it was the school administration and particularly Father Regi Mathew.

He was known in the school as the Child that Father Regi Mathew did not have. Such was the bond between them. Being the head of an institution such as the one that Father Regi Mathew ran and being a surrogate father to not only Rohit but scores of other children like him was not only a challenge but also taxing. Especially when you have a born to create trouble child, like Rohit. Being a man of the cloth, Father Regi Mathew was a devout Christian who took it upon himself that it was the will of God that brought these children under this care and tutelage. Otherwise, he reasoned, what were the chances of these children born to different parents – some from half way across the world – to be brought under his care, if it were not for Divine Will. And so, he accepted that responsibility and although he was supposed to be a strict disciplinarian – he was also a kind soul whose gaze, whose very countenance announced his kindness like some printed Halo affixed to the high walls of the Chapel in the campus.

The child was getting into some fracas or the other. All that happened in the moments that he was left unsupervised. It was almost as if Rohit Das Gupta was fine in the class room, he would study well, get good grades was really a 'a good student' but on the other hand was this absolute rascal who somehow transformed into this trouble hunting madness.

As the years passed, after many hours of counselling and kindly spoken lectures, Rohit improved. Unfortunately, the improvement would last only a few hours or at best a few days. Out of supervisory Circle of Control – Rohit Das Gupta would spring up like the proverbial jack in the box – with a vengeance.

There right under the watchful guidance of the entire staff and fraternity – developed a typical Jekyl and Hyde character and if anyone was born to trouble other people with his or her presence in the world – Rohit Das Gupta would top the charts.

About the time he'd got into the elementary school his father became a little more powerful than he already was by getting into mainstream politics. In the twilight of the industrial revolution that had swept into this country where factories came up almost like overnight mushrooms, a new political leadership was also born. These new leaders came not from the hangover of the independence era – the freedom fighters and their ilk – but from rough neighbourhoods and fiercely fought battles. They were divided over caste, creed, religion and Union rather than Nation or any such lofty ideals.

There used to be a time when Politics was fought, yes – but with veiled gloves and metaphor enriched debates. Now the gloves were off and it was brutal sledging on the sidelines and in the main stream. Nothing was sacrosanct and there was no quart taken and none given. It seemed like that there was a time when politics was about the important matters of Nation building and dialogue with all concerned, almost as if it was like some quaint club cricket gentleman's game.

Not anymore. Das Gupta Senior's arrival into politics heralded a new era where the rough and tough mingled with 'politics in my blood' kind of veterans. Street fighter was the new nomenclature that was added to the already descriptive aliases and nom de guerre that these politicians adopted for themselves. This characteristic attracted to them many followers and thus a new eco system began to prevail.

There were musclemen – like your club bouncers – who were there for their muscle power, trained to look menacing and tough – the first line of defence for these politicos or their first line of deterrent – depending on who you were. Then there were the retired bureaucrats and 'intellectuals' – those who knew the system, its inner intricacies and its workings and those who could be fronted to businessmen and corporates should they need lobbying within the government, should policies be made or framed or avoided.

Then there was another layer of semi criminals who existed on the threshold of the law but didn't hesitate to step into the netherworld of criminals and the illegal. You could spot them a mile away from their flashy jewellery, trademark religious brandishing's – a bright red tilak that ran from between the eyes to the top of the head like some garish neon sign made the person look even more furtive than he already was. Or it was a taawis around the neck, kohl in the eyes and a skull cap parked perilously on the back of the head. Or a big cross crusted with fake American diamonds embellished with blue and green stones nestling between building chest muscles meant to make it look like emeralds and sapphires. Parked under these folks were a bevy of high school drop outs, the nearly went to jail types, the minor cons and the desperados who were basically hired goons who rented out their services to the most convenient employer.

Thanks to an ever-wakeful media – those that were clearly defined as criminals didn't consort with these politicians openly, they were managed or communicated through this intermediaries and handlers.

Whenever Rohit came home for a vacation or to spend time with his parents – these days it was never together with both his parents – he would stay with his mother who was, by now, given the official status of second wife and therefore some respectability. He would visit his father and spend some time with him. The conversations between them were not of the greatest – just a few questions about his studies, his school life, his well being and that was that. Of course, Das Gupta's first wife knew about Rohit and his mother and unlike what one see's in the media and in the gossip columns – there wasn't any rancour or animosity between the spouses of one man. Sometimes there was downright acceptance of the second wife's existence and if that wasn't there – there was a grudging respect. But no cat fights and Machiavellian plotting to edge one another out of the equation. So Rohit did mingle with his step brothers and sister – to a certain extent. Sometimes they would all land up together in one car when they went on an outing with their father.

It is complicated to explain this to someone who is from a completely different cultural background. There was a time in this country when one had a second wife or a mistress it was a sign of one's economic prowess. It was a social status. Perhaps the acceptance came down from years of the Royals having huge harems? It wasn't isolated and it wasn't considered obscene to have two wives or even more. Now thanks to an all-pervading social media access to members of the opposite sex wasn't hard to come by.

Rohit Das Gupta, somehow, blended in with the ease of a chameleon into his father's organization. He made friends easily. Partially because of the fact that he was the boss's son and secondly – he was easy to befriend. He smoked with those that didn't dare to see eye to eye with his father. With the very senior one's he even drank a beer or two with them. When they talked shop, he would eagerly listen in with deep enthusiasm.

For someone who was just in high school, Rohit looked much older than his age. He had the physique of a twenty something year old young man. That was partially due to the fact that Father Regi Mathew had particularly instructed the PT teacher, Cliff Dawson to train the boy. The very English looking down to the deep blue grey eyes – PT Teacher Cliff Dawson was of Anglo Indian descent but for the sake of convenience and self esteem he preferred to only exhibit his English ancestry and spoke very little of his Indian side. Cliff Dawson was unsparingly tough on his students inside his little forte. The Gymnasium. When he was specifically instructed by Father Regi Mathew to pay special attention to one of the students – Cliff Dawson did exactly that.

Rohit had been under Cliff Dawson's personal attention for almost 5 years and as he reached adolescence the boys physique was showing proof of the exacting gym schedule that he was subject to.

Cliff Dawson was also a mixed martial arts teacher and when he took Rohit into the ring to spar, he wasn't kind. Perhaps Father Regi Mathew knew that boys like Rohit needed a good hiding to be properly disciplined and wrought into the makings of a Regi Mathew product? No one really knew. But Cliff Dawson was never openly questioned for the treatment that was meted out either inside the ring or for that matter inside the gymnasium by anyone, least of all Father Regi Mathew.

So much so that by this time Rohit Das Gupta was looking like a physically toned, self-assured, slightly cocky but in a handsome model sort of way young man. He had developed a John Travoltaesque kind of strut which he'd seen in an old film of the actors called Saturday Night Fever. He fell in love with that character and often chose to express himself in exactly the same manner.

Plus, it also suited his own self image that he'd created about himself. The martial arts training – although it was punishing and at times brutal – helped him to see himself in a better image. He was certainly no wimp and he made sure that everyone who confronted him knew that. His skirmishes increased with classmates and even some of the school staff, but by the end of it – they knew that Rohit Das Gupta was no push over.

When he landed up in his father's territory – this avatar that was Rohit Das Gupta was accepted as the real Thing. An almost unwitting coronation of the Heir to the Boss. Although in the company of people from the lowest strata of society, Rohit was amidst people who sensed a great deal more than they let up. Street smart survivors who crawled up from dingy places that most of us would never ever survive in – these men knew a Man a mile away. They defined their future interactions, their respect and their solidarity with that reading they'd initially made.

Rohit was given that respect they attributed to only those that 'fit the bill.' And he fit the bill to the hilt.

Girls were attracted to him like flies to a sweet meat stall by the road side and his sexcapades were the stories that bordered on the ludicrous. And like always there were fights because of the girls – for Rohit there was absolutely no issue when he befriended a girl despite being told she was with someone else or for that matter engaged or even married!

By the time he'd passed high school, two things happened. Father Regi Mathew who had held his hand and virtually brought him up from almost the time he was a baby, passed away in his sleep. It was a moment that Rohit wouldn't ever forget in his entire life. He felt a vacuum that he'd never ever felt in his life. Whatever the fracas that he got into, he knew that Father Regi would admonish him. But he also knew that Father Regi Mathew would eventually throw his arms round Rohit's shoulder and almost say in that one gesture – "You are a rascal, but I love you."

His father would never replace Father Regi Mathew and there would be no other person in Rohit's life who'd ever come close to understanding his soul like Father Regi Mathew had.

By the time he'd moved out of the hostel and high school that was his entire existence till then – his mother was detected with cancer. It was too late to do anything about it. But then his mother was stoic just as she'd been about everything else in her life. She'd mellowed down considerably after Rohit's birth and never got involved in either Union Politics or public life actively. She let Das Gupta take the glare of the centre stage and left it at that.

She'd become drawn to the local ISKCON temple and that was where most of her energies were directed almost the entire time that Rohit was in the care of the Jesuit Brothers and his hostel. Perhaps when you change the environment there are subtle changes in your life that also becomes apparent. That firebrand Union worker was now a soft spoken, bhajan seeking ISKCON devotee whose kindness and charity was highly appreciated and heard about.

Disease, however, isn't very choosy about who to attack, when or where. And it did claim its umpteenth victim in Rohit's mother.

She didn't suffer though. From the day she was diagnosed with 4th stage of adenocarcinoma or stomach cancer till the day she died – exactly one month after the diagnosis was made – she was constantly surrounded by friends and her own family on a daily basis from early morning till late evening. There would be impromptu bhajan singing sessions, there would be the joyous laughter of a reunion of old friends – this throng of friends and well-wishers and family was a testimony to the life she'd lead.

Das Gupta too was there – whenever time permitted. Rohit was by now staying with her – so he too was there.

Finally she passed away one glorious summer day almost like none other. The wreaths that were brought for Rohit's mother was not in any small quantity. Cutting across political lines, family and her ISKCON Family members were all present to bid her final farewell.

Lighting the funeral pyre as the only son, he showed his defiance to the very end. He refused to shave his hair off. Finally the elders relented and got him to the cemetery to light the pyre. He arrived there with a few of his father's trusted lieutenants – high on weed and liquor.

Not many noticed though, while he hurriedly finished off the formalities of the funeral and rushed back into the car to be whisked home.

He was not very close to his mother – but somewhere over a period of time – his mother had mellowed considerably and perhaps was a little more humane than her original self. Perhaps that touched Rohit, perhaps maternal love has this armour piercing quality that afflicts us all? In a twisted and warped way Rohit learnt kindness from her – which was a far cry from his father's way of life, his trappings and his never say die hunger for power.

College was another tumultuous journey and his escapades only increased. Fights were routine, his acceptance into his father's non- political side grew and people were already accepting Rohit Das Gupta to be the sole heir to his father's political and Union legacy.

Seasons change and so does time. The factories were now almost rid of militant unions and their firebrand leadership. Partnerships were in place, a new dawn was being heralded and by the time Rohit finished with college, there was a complete new generation looking ahead to a new country.

His father was still into active politics and had become a mass leader of some appeal. Because of the fact that Rohit liked being in the humdrum of politics – he began to take over the day-to-day back office management. He loved the attention and to his mind, he was a similar avatar of the Godfather character in that timeless classic movie. There were times when he emulated either Marlon Brando or even Kamal Hassan in that desi Godfather type of movie. He was the go-to man for

Justice for all the people whom the Law would never even pay heed to. He was the local protector from other local thugs and muscles. He was the sole Protection from the law, and al rowdyism and it wasn't long before people actually started calling him Chottae Dada. It was his father who was called Dada and there'd be no replacing that. Rohit was Chottae Dada and he loved it that way and made no move to correct anyone who called him so

Girl friends, affairs and such relationships were now commonplace in Rohit's life and it wasn't long that he was not actually in some relationship or the other. Being a regular at the watering holes in the city, he knew most of the high flying crowd.

That is how he met Helen. She was with a few people and she was the only other woman in that group. She was smiling and flirtatious and she was sending out so much of raw sexual energy that almost everyone noticed her.

Rohit was attracted to such energy without a moment's hesitation and it wasn't long before he caught her eye, smiled at her and then asked her over to his table.

To say that Rohit fell for Helen would be an understatement. He'd had his share of girl friends, sexual partners and what have you. But he'd never been in love.

All that changed when he fell for Helen, completely smitten by her, besotted by her charm. It wasn't long before he became, her protector and mentor, lover and boy friend.

Fast forward to today at the conference where Helen died – they'd almost been living together.

When she told him that she'd be gone for a couple of days at a company organized conference, he too decided to go and although they were staying in separate rooms – almost everyone knew that Rohit Das Gupta, officially Helen's close male friend was also staying there.

For Inspector Pratap Rao Singh, Rohit Das Gupta happened to be the new trump card who had all the trappings of being a first class suspect in the murder of Helen.

❑❑❑

Chapter 9: Senior Inspector Pratap Rao Singh

To be present at a murder scene from the moment an investigation begins and to be in the presence of the exact crowd where the victim was present in was both a blessing and to some extent a frustration.

One had to unravel a lot of the necessary and the unnecessary.

For that one needed to be possessed of some God given acumen, professional experience and an unerring instinct that was guided by a brain that never lost sight of the target.

In this case the target was not to prove one's Supreme Investigative capabilities. It was to destroy the confidence of a murderer or murderers, as the case might be, and to expose their heinous intention and then to book them for murder.

That was clear in the mind of Inspector Pratap Rao Singh, for sure. There was no ego here. There was no superiority complex at play. Just a hard-nosed police professional at the top of his game. Combined with his deep interest – and of course his education in human psychology – the policeman's intent was high powered by some innate self confidence that was hard to push asunder.

The "Usual Suspects" were at hand. Although he spoke to many of the staff present at the venue – he'd only be impressed by the few that he'd had detailed discussions with and who are mentioned here in this case diary.

From the beginning of his tenure in the police force, then being promoted to Senior P.I. he'd always felt that there was some Divine Grace that was always by him, prompting him to see things that others missed completely. Providing him with insights that shocked the others – almost as if he'd had some insider information that was impossible to get. Plus his education – something that he cherished very much and which he believed helped him unravel the cleverly constructed narratives of suspects – plus his knowledge of Palmistry which he'd learnt from his father – all created a formidable investigator of the highest order.

Thus, blessed with a keen eye for the most minute of details, he began to review his case diary, revisiting the statements and observations that had caught his attention. He had a knack for separating fact from fiction, and his experience told him that the key to solving the case lay in the subtle inconsistencies and contradictions that often went unnoticed by less seasoned investigators.

As he delved deeper into the case file, Singh's mind raced with theories and hypotheses. He knew that the killer was likely still in the vicinity, watching and waiting to see if their crime would go undetected. Singh's determination to uncover the truth was unwavering, driven by a strong sense of justice and a desire to bring closure to the victim's loved ones.

With a deep breath, Singh made a mental note to re-interview a few key witnesses and to follow up on some promising leads. He was convinced that the breakthrough he needed was just around the corner, and his instincts told him that the identification of the killer was closer than they thought.

What was left behind? What was necessary to nab the murderer? How was it that everyone was so cool about the whole incident?

In that moment he felt a rather deep sadness for Helen. Someone working with the most confidential of the highest office in the organization, someone who was literally scrabbling to make a living – not just for herself but for her ailing mother as well. Someone who played the organizational politics to the hilt, almost as if she was the orchestrator of the entire play. Helen in a manner of speaking was cunning, vicious and completely focused on achieving her goals – no matter what anyone thought of her, no matter how she managed to achieve those goals.

Yet despite all the Machiavellian games she'd played in the end she'd lost everything and gained nothing. Her post mortem was carried out post haste – and a prima facie case of murder by poison was established by the pathologist. A more detailed study of the report would entail – but this was enough. This was no accident. It was a brutal murder. Conceptualized by someone very clever. Someone who was confident that it would never come to light. Someone who thought that the Senior management would pay off the cops and brush this under the carpet. After all – these things were common. No one in their right minds wanted a scandal. Especially in a company where things were going well, the owners didn't have to sweat the small stuff to live a more than comfortable lifestyle. The person who died was 'hired help' – nothing to worry about. There'd be no tall claims to settle, there'd be no press to manage. Sure, there'd be the rag tag journalism sniffing a scandal, a major scoop or a cover up – but those things could be managed. But it was imperative to close this sordid chapter. Quickly.

So the calls had been made. To the highest authorities and they put the pressure on Senior Police Inspector Pratap Rao Singh to close the case and vacate the premises.

Day Three of the murder and still there was just 'discussions' with the staff and some personal notes that was being made. No arrests. No suspects. Police HO was increasing the pressure. Till now there was no press. No celebrity involved. Well, Shubodh Das Gupta's son wasn't exactly a celebrity!

Pratap Rao Singh had sent his personal driver home and picked up some clothes from his almirah. That's how he'd survived being offsite these couple of days. That is all that he'd given himself leeway – three to four days and he'd be gone by then.

Apart from this murder investigation there was also other routine things that needed his attention.

He'd parked himself in one of the rooms and that was now the nerve centre of the investigation, where he sat at his make shift desk, sipping his tea and staring at the investigation report in front of him. Helen's case was proving to be a tough nut to crack. No leads, no suspects, no motive. Just a mysterious poisoning that had claimed her life.

He rubbed his temples, feeling the fatigue of the past few days. His team had been working around the clock, but they had nothing concrete to show for it.

Just then, his phone rang. It was the forensic lab. "Inspector, we've found something interesting," the voice on the other end said. "Helen's phone records show a number that keeps popping up in the days leading up to her death. It's a payphone in the city."

Pratap Rao Singh's ears perked up. A payphone? Who used those anymore? "Get me the location," he said, his mind racing with possibilities.

He picked up his mobile phone and called for his jeep and when his driver brought it around – he headed out to investigate. The payphone was located in a seedy part of town, the kind of place where only shady deals went down. The drive out of the resort was also much needed. He realized one thing – everything good can turn very bad if it's not in a limit. People paid good money to spend time in a resort – but you couldn't live there for ever. The food, the bed, the view – all became monotonous and boring.

He pushed those thoughts out of his mind. His heart raced as he approached the phone booth. Who had Helen been talking to? And what did it have to do with her murder?

As Singh approached the payphone, he noticed a man lurking in the shadows, eyeing him with a mix of curiosity and suspicion. The man was tall, with a gaunt face and sunken eyes that seemed to bore into his soul.

Pratap Rao Singh's instincts kicked in, and he quickly surveyed the area, his eyes scanning for any potential threats. The man seemed to be alone, but he couldn't shake off the feeling that the man was hiding something.

"Can I help you?" came that policeman's trained voice - firm but polite.

The man hesitated, then stepped forward, his eyes darting back and forth. "I was just... uh... making a call," he stammered.

Pratap Rao Singh's eyes narrowed. "At a payphone? In this part of town?"

The man shrugged, his eyes avoiding the policeman's searing gaze. "I was just passing by."

Singh's gut told him that this man was hiding something. He quickly pulled out his notebook and began to ask questions, his eyes locked on the man's shifty gaze.

"Come here." This was that brusque no-nonsense voice that Pratap Rao Singh used when he wanted things to happen. There was no quarter given. Only one expectation. That the order be obeyed.

The man came over. He smelt of sweat and cheap liquor. He looked like the thousands if not millions of nameless, faceless wasted human existence that existed in the city . Their addiction justified, they wasted away their lives with daily dosages into oblivion. They were not too averse to doing something – even though it might have a touch of risk to it – if that would fruition into fuelling their drug or alcohol purchase.

As the man came closer, he noticed a faint tattoo on his wrist - a small snake coiled around a sword. Singh's mind raced back to the case files, and he remembered a similar tattoo mentioned in one of the witness statements.

"Where did you get that tattoo?" Singh asked, his voice firm but controlled.

When you are asked with an uncomfortable question there is a tendency to answer the question with another question.

The man's eyes widened, and he took a step back, his eyes darting around the area nervously. "I... uh... got it from a friend," he stammered.

The Policeman's eyes narrowed. "What's your name?" he asked, his hand reaching for his handcuffs.

The man hesitated, then mumbled something under his breath. Singh's ears perked up - it sounded like "Rajesh" or "Rajeev".

Just then, the Inspector's phone rang. He answered it, his eyes still locked on the suspicious man. "Inspector, we've found something," a colleague said. "A security camera caught a glimpse of someone that could be the killer, and we managed to enhance the image. It looks like... ".

His heart raced as he listened to the description. It sounded like the man standing in front of him.

Just then there was a blip and Senior Inspector Pratap Rao Singh's phone went dead. In sheer frustration he nearly threw it out.

The drunk was bundled into the back of the Bolero Police jeep and they drove back fast to the resort to continue the investigation.

A light at the end of the Investigation Tunnel.

When an offer was made to the suspect who was picked up near the pay phone to eat a meal, have a bath or something more to drink – he happily took all three.

A fresh room was opened for the resorts newest occupant. A drunk picked up from the streets of this sprawling city, now a full-fledged suspect.

Once freshened up, with a heavy breakfast in his stomach and nice cold glass of whisky in his hands, the drunk began to speak.

The details were blurred to Pratap Rao Singh's mind, he had asked for a police stenographer to be present at the site for documenting these statements. One had reached the resort just that morning. So he knew that the notes would be taken. He was looking for a clue. A motive. Something that would point the investigation to the murderer.

One thing he was sure of. This drunk wasn't the murderer. He might have played a part. But that was all. He was an accessory after the fact. But he wasn't the murderer. He was too soft. Too much of a drunk.

Most of it was a rambling about his being drunk. About how he started to drink. About how he was kicked out of his comfortable home.

Just when he was about to get bored and call off this interview, the drunk mentioned one name.

Senior Inspector Pratap Rao Singh almost jumped.

"..............Shubodh Das Gupta..." He heard from the drunk.

"What about Shubodh Das Gupta?" Singh asked him, standing over the drunk like some towering colossus.

"He came over a few days to where we normally hang out." The drunk said.

"He spoke to a few friends of mine. Bought them some booze. Food. Got them interested in whatever he was talking about." The drunk continued.

"Then on the third or the fourth time that he was there along with what seemed to be his sidekick or driver – I don't know which – one of my friends brought me into the august company that he was keeping – with Shubodh Das Gupta." The drunk reminisced.

"There was something to be done. Something that would be 'no problem' and if done well – it would mean a payout of some substantial amount." He told the policeman.

Now that he'd got one name out of the man's mouth, he knew that the rest of the stuff that he had to share could be handled by his deputy.

So he called his deputy who was in the vicinity and told him to take the drunk outside and talk to him. Then he said, almost as an after thought, "I think that labour union leader's son is also in the resort. Rohit Das Gupta is his name. Go upto the reception and check which room he's in. Then go there and ask Rohit to come up here to meet with me." Pratap Rao Singh instruction were crisp and left no doubt in the mind of the other policeman.

When Rohit came up to meet Pratap Rao Singh, the two sized each other up. Within the shortest time span, Rohit gave way. He grasped that much about Pratap Rao Singh's demeanour and manner immediately. This was no push over. This was no stooge. He wouldn't bend down for anyone. No point calling anyone to get them to speak to this policeman.

Pratap Rao Singh approached Rohit, his eyes narrowing as he took in the young man's confident demeanor. Or was it just a mask to conceal the fear that anyone feels in the company of a policeman?

"Rohit Das Gupta, I need to ask you some questions," he said, his voice firm but polite.

Rohit raised an eyebrow but nodded amiably. "Of course, Inspector. What's this about?"

Singh pulled out his notebook. "Helen's murder. I understand you were close to her?"

Rohit's expression turned sombre. "Yes, we were. We'd been together for a few months. But I didn't kill her, if that's what you're implying."

Singh's eyes locked onto Rohit's. "I'm not thinking anything yet, Mr. Das Gupta. But I do need to ask you some questions. Can you tell me where you were last few days? Especially on the morning that Helen died?

Rohit thought for a moment before responding. "I was at a friend's party. We were celebrating his birthday. I left around 12:30 am and then came back to my room, here in this resort. I did not meet with Helen here in the resort, privately, if that is what you mean? She knew I was there, we exchanged a few whatsapp messages, I told her that we could stay here a couple of days after her Conference ended. She just sent me back a smiley, let's see she'd said."

Was there a hint of sadness in his voice, Pratap Rao Singh wondered, when Rohit spoke about Helen?

Singh's eyes never left Rohit's face. "Can anyone confirm your alibi?"

Rohit nodded. "Yes, my friend Rajiv was with me the whole time. And the hotel's CCTV will show me entering my room around 12:45 am."

Pratap Rao Singh made a mental note of that. Here was a man who knew that there were CCTV cameras installed, could he have deliberately made himself visible to those camera's just to create his own alibi?

He made a point of making a note in his book. "I'll need to speak with Rajiv and see the hotel's footage." He told Rohit.

Then he pulled out his phone and showed Rohit a photo of the drunk who was now in the resort as a 'guest of the police'.

"Have you seen this man before Rohit?" Pratap Rao Singh asked him, watching him closely for his response.

"Who is he?" Rohit asked.

"Never mind who he is. Do you know this man or have you seen him before?" The policeman's voice came back on, the niceties were over.

Rohit shook his head negatively, pursing his lips. Almost trying to recall. He was supposedly instrumental in managing the back end of his father's constituency, or so he liked to think. But there were others, dedicated to his father – who ran the entire back office. They were survivors, who knew their locus standi. They didn't dare to take the limelight. In the limelight was Rohit Bhaiyya. Their front man. They did everything behind that protective veneer of his image.

"OK Rohit Das Gupta, you can leave for now. But don't leave the city. Don't disappear on one of your jaunts. Understood?" The Policeman asked.

Rohit's face relaxed, and he smiled. "Thanks, Inspector. I am at your disposal. " He mockly curtsied and made his exit as if from some royal presence.

But Singh's eyes lingered on Rohit's face, his mind still turning over the evidence. Was Rohit telling the truth, or was he hiding something?

He knew that he'd have to travel to the city to meet with Rohit's father. Shubodh Das Gupta was a man with a reputation for 'managing' bureaucrats, politicians, the system and that is why he was where is today. Being in the rough and tumble of union politics for almost 4 decades, climbing to its very zenith from the pits of being a daily wage labourer, doing the most menial jobs is quite a heady journey.

This wasn't a man to mess with. There were tales of the people who'd tried to mess with him and who were now reticent onlookers to his amazing growth or simply moved out of town and stayed out.

He couldn't help but wonder about Shubodh Das Gupta's involvement in Helen's murder. He knew that Shubodh was a powerful man with many enemies, and that he had a reputation for ruthlessness in his business dealings.

Singh decided to pay Shubodh a visit, to see if he could uncover any information that might lead him to the killer. As he arrived at Shubodh's office, he was greeted by a stern-looking secretary who told him that Shubodh was busy, but would see him shortly.

Singh waited for several minutes before Shubodh emerged from his office, a tall, imposing figure with a stern expression.

"What do you want, Inspector?" Shubodh asked gruffly with the least amount of civility in his voice.

Singh stood up straight, meeting Shubodh's gaze. "I'm investigating a murder, Mr. Das Gupta. I wanted to talk to you with regards to that case."

Shubodh's expression darkened. "What are you insinuating, Inspector?"

Singh held his ground. "I'm not insinuating anything, Mr. Das Gupta. I'm just trying to get to the truth. Do you know Helen, a lady who is intimate with your son?"

Shubodh snorted. "My son has a lot of girlfriends. Maybe she is one of them?" He sneered.

Singh's eyes narrowed. "You approve of that?"

Shubodh leaned back in his chair, steepling his fingers together. "Kids these days," he almost sighed. "Nothing we say makes any sense to them, nothing they do makes any sense to us. So best is to let them do what they want to do. That is how I manage my boy, Inspector."

Shubodh is being evasive and dismissive, the policeman knew it in his gut. But this was not the time to give up. He knew that too. When you put someone in an uncomfortable position the mind plays tricks. The bravado confidence goes for a toss, the truth fights to be told and finally what emerges is how most whodunnits are solved.

Something cracks. Something gives way. You cannot hide the truth.

"What do you know about Helen's murder, Mr. Das Gupta?" Singh asks, his eyes locked on Shubodh's face.

Shubodh shrugs. "Nothing, Inspector. I've already told you; I just know that Rohit was going around with her. I also told you that Rohit has other girlfriends too."

The Policeman then decided to change tracks. "I think you're being economical with the truth Mr. Das Gupta. And I'm going to find out what it is."

Shubodh sneered at him. "You're wasting your time, Inspector. I'm a respected businessman and politician. I have nothing to hide."

The tension between them is palpable. Shubodh's expression darkens, but Singh doesn't back down easily. He's determined to get to the truth, no matter what it takes.

"I can make one call and have you transferred to some place where they don't even have a table for you to sit." Shubodh Das Gupta openly threatened the policeman.

Pratap Rao Singh smiled grimly. In his career, he'd heard this one line several times. He wasn't afraid of these threats. He wasn't about to be threatened either. "We'll see about that. I'll investigate every aspect of your life, Mr. Das Gupta. And if I find out that you're involved in Helen's murder, you'll be the one who's wasting time - in prison."

Singh's eyes never left Shubodh's face, his mind racing with possibilities. He knew that Shubodh was hiding something, but he needed concrete evidence to prove it.

"I'll need a list of your employees and associates, Mr. Das Gupta," Singh said, his voice firm but polite. "And I'll need to speak with your son, Rohit, again. This time, in your presence."

Shubodh's expression turned cold, but he nodded curtly. "Very well, Inspector. I'll have my secretary prepare the list. And I'll call Rohit in when you want to speak to him next. Is that all?"

Singh's eyes scanned the office, taking in the lavish decorations and the stunning view of the city skyline. He knew that Shubodh's wealth and influence were formidable, but he was determined to uncover the truth.

He picked up his notes, his phone and he turned to leave the presence of Shubodh Das Gupta. "Thank you for your time, Mr. Das Gupta. I will take your leave." He walked towards the door.

With his hands on the door, Senior Police Inspector Pratap Rao Singh, turned almost as if he'd forgotten something.

Shubodh Das Gupta was also watching the policeman leave and when the policeman turned suddenly at the door, he caught Shubodh's gaze.

Singh's eyes narrowed. "I clean forgot something." He said and walked back to the table where Mr. Das Gupta was sitting at.

"How come Helen's phone records show multiple calls to and from your official number in the days leading up to her murder?" Pratap Rao Singh put his palms on the table and leaned forward towards Shubodh Das Gupta almost waiting for him to answer the question.

Both the men looked at each other, finally Mr. Das Gupta said, "Rohit also uses this office, and since you say that they were having an affair, he might have called her. Did you check with him? If not, you do that." He waved the policeman almost dismissively and got up to leave the room from the door behind his chair.

The room fell silent, and Pratap Rao Singh knew he had hit a nerve.

❑❑❑

Chapter 10: A Sinister Plan

A few months ago Shubodh Das Gupta discovered he had a problem. His son Rohit Das Gupta was seeing a new girl. That didn't surprise him. Rohit's amorous life had made its mark ever since he was in high school. What he did was etched in the fathers mind. Those days things were different. There wasn't this every snooping social media to deal with. Times were different. Then there was the shelter of long drawn cases, courts and the whole nine yards! Now? The damn media conducted a kangaroo trial and before you knew it – heads rolled.

But Shubodh da – as he was fondly referred to or Dada – wasn't a man that let small issues deter him. They were nipped very efficiently in the bud. He ensured that they didn't let him bother him to the extent that he'd fret and fume and let that Inner Peace within him fritter away to sleepless nights and a certain uneasiness.

That day he sat in his plush office, sipping his tea and gazing out the window at the bustling city below. His mind was focused on the problem at hand: Helen and her relationship with his son, Rohit. He couldn't let that continue. The boy was getting serious. He'd told a few Trojan Horses that he'd planted within the boys circle of friends – people who'd report to him every single move that Rohit made. Shubodh da justified that – 'just for his protection' an early warning system to take care of things before they snowballed into unmanageable situations. Be they unwanted pregnancies in Rohit's several girl friends over the years, be it a debt that was taken with the promise to returned in a few days. Whatever the issue – they were dealt with almost like some juggernaut that cleared the path.

There were these Janta Durbars that Shubodh da conducted every week. In these Durbars his office was thrown open to the general public. People from all walks would come in to meet him. They'd have written petitions addressed to him as their sitting MLA. It would be usually for some assistance in securing an admission to a school or a college. Otherwise it would be for financial assistance to overcome some crisis or the other. Else it would be a 'humble request' to Shubodh Da to preside in a dispute over some legacy property and settle it. Often such invitations resulted in Shubodh Da acquiring the property at some ridiculous price. Such acquired properties were now a major asset bank in Shubodh Das Gupta's veritable economic power.

There were discreet requests to take care of. These would be to interfere in meting out justice to some aggrieved parties who weren't satisfied with the judicial systems interpretation of justice. One nod of Shubodh Da's head would mean the end of a life. Such was his power. People knew it. They respected that power because he rarely misused it. You cannot be a Union Leader for ages and then graduate to an MLA without some empathy quotient.

On one of these days, his close associate from several years – who just like him had moved from the hustle and bustle of Union work into mainstream politics – walked into his office and wanted a word with him.

For such "private meetings" he moved into an ante chamber adjoining to his office and it was a cozy small office which consisted of a throne like single seater sofa in front of which were two other small three seaters where the visitors were seated. It was completely glassed, air-conditioned and you could not bring in your phone here.

His associate bowed down and touched his feet. This was a traditional token of respect. Not mandatory. But it was expected.

"Theek hai, theek hai ," Shubodh Da touched the other man's bowed head with a smile. Deep down he wondered what brought the man to his office. That too in the middle of a Janta Durbar.

He didn't waste any time. He asked the other man. "Tell me, what brings you here." He asked looking at the man straight in the eye.

"Ek important matter hai." The man began, his eyes now

downcast. Not looking at the powerful aura that Shubodh Da emitted.

"A man in my area had come to me. He's working with some important people. He's been there in that company for many years." The man explained.

"What's it got to do with me?" Shubodh Da asked him, now rather puzzled. Often small matters were never brought to his attention, they were taken care of at a lower level. The people who constituted his lower echelon in his organization – both the labour union and the political apparatus – were staunch loyalists. They'd kill in his name. They'd earned their place in these organizations after they were proven. They'd have been tested sometime or the other in their careers. Shubodh Da didn't value anything more than Loyalty. And his kind of Loyalty was a no questions asked blind loyalty. These followers were men and women and even children from the lowest strata of society. They had nothing. Least of all any prestige that would take a beating if they'd land up on the wrong side of the law – for example. The height of recognition of being a Shubodh Das Gupta loyalist was a small office in a particular area. Just a small place, in the middle of a working class extremely blue collar area – the sign board had a picture of Shubodh Das Gupta and the occupant of that office – smiling at each other in deep faith.

That was enough. To get there meant a certain recognition. In that area. To be counted as one of the Lieutenants of Shubodh

Das Gupta was as certain as being Blessed by a God that no one had seen. For the mere mortals Shubodh Das Gupta was that God which answered their slightest prayers, he made their homes possible, he was the one who got their children into schools they'd otherwise never be admitted into.

Now parked into his chair inside the ante chamber, Shubodh asked him again, "Ha, tell me what is this matter. I have people waiting for me since morning. Make it quick."

"This man, this employee had some problem with a local girl." He explained wringing his hands almost as if he was to blame.

"What did he do?" Shubodh asked.

"He played around with her. Till now it was not really problematic. It was just being a sugar daddy. But when the opportunity arose, he got physical. Nothing serious. Just touching her. Petting her. That kind of stuff Dada. That girl also didn't say anything. Her silence got this man a little bolder. He took her in his car and went outside of town and in some secluded place he had sex with the girl." The man explained.

"Now this man discovers that the girl is pregnant Dada. There is a problem. The girl is under age. If the news gets out he will be finished." The man explained.

"The bloody idiot spends so much on a little pip squeak of a girl and he couldn't afford a condom for himself? The miser needs to be hung by his balls." Shubodh Das Gupta almost spat out.

"He came to me Dada when the girl told him that she was pregnant. He immediately told her that he'd stand by her and see to it that she got an abortion done. Now she says she told her mother and that the mother wanted to see this man." The visitor explained.

"Ah, this is getting interesting." Shubodh Das Gupta almost smiled!

"The meeting between this officer and the mother happened. The mother realized that her daughter had reeled in a big fish. A fish that couldn't afford a scandal. A fish that could be milked quite well. Perhaps milked enough so that the girl could be married off to some fellow from their village and sent away? The mothers mouth had begun to water at the thought even as her daughter contritely explained her predicament to the mother." The man explained.

"The man agreed Dada. He said what are you looking for? The mother told him something astronomical. He cannot afford that kind of money Dada. He asked the mother to re-think the number. But she was adamant. She said either you pay or I go to the police and file a rape case. She seems to know everything Dada. The girl is underage. The man could be booked under the POCSO Act Dada. That happens and its over for him. His family life will collapse. His life, his career, his standing in society – everything collapses Dada." The man pleaded almost as if it was his brother for whom he was speaking.

"What is the number she quoted?" Shubodh Da asked the man.

"She is asking for 25 lakhs of rupees Dada. She says its reasonable considering what the man will lose." The man said.

"What do you want me to do in this matter?" Shubodh Da asked the visitor.

"Dada you just need to tell me and I will handle the matter in the manner in which you guide me." The man said in prayerful worship.

"How affluent is this man?" Shubodh Da asked.

"Dada he's the Purchase Manager in a very large organization. He's a trusted man of the organization's owners, he's been there for a long time. He's quite a senior manager. But he's not rich that way." The man explained.

"Arrey, these fellows working in these organizations are the richest. What do you know? Those days are gone when the Zamindar's family were the richest. Or the fellow with the largest foundry was the rich man. Now? These glass buildings that house some of the largest organizations in the world have people whose salaries are astronomical." Shubodh Da told his underling.

"I think that mother is someone who we need to meet. She's the kind of sharpness that we need in our organization. Just imagine her guts. Her daughter is a victim. Yet, see her mentality. You, my dear daughter, are doomed. For a few trinkets you sold your virginity. But darling – you brought me a bonanza with your sacrifice. Even the Goddess wouldn't have blessed me so despite all the prayers and sacrifices I have made for her over the years." Shubodh Da mimicked a female voice almost as if he was impersonating the conversation between the mother and the daughter.

It seemed to the visitor that the matter was now completely out of his hands. He thought that Shubodh Da would tell him, with that famous wave of the hand, to 'take care of the matter'. But now he seemed to be suggesting that the mother should be inducted into the Shubodh Das Gupta Organization!

"I will do one thing, since you have personally invested your energies into this matter." Shubodh Da said almost gently to the man.

"Yes Dada." The hands were wringing into each other.

"What is the name of the man who screwed this girl?" Shubodh Da asked the man.

"Dada his name is Shyam Maheshwari." The man volunteered the information. "He's actually a good supporter Dada. Makes some donations personally to our organization, then he gets his company waala's to donate money when we go there for donations. He's a good man. What to do Dada, his time is bad, that's all." The man tried to explain.

"That rascal's insatiable desire landed him into trouble. Not his time. His time is excellent. He got you to fight for him na?" Shubodh Da shot back. With that one sentence he told the man – "I Know that you have charged Shyam Maheshwari a small fee for representing his case to me."

"Dada you have taught us well na? We have to serve the aggrieved public." The man said his eyes cast down.

Shubodh Da looked at the man. Was he making fun or was he serious?

"Do one thing. Bring that fellow to me. Let me speak to him. Then we will decide how to close this matter."

"Dada he's come with me." The man said.

"Ask him to come inside. I have no time. There are many people waiting outside. You saw that." Shubodh Das Gupta showed the man his impatience.

The man got up and went outside.

The door opened, and Shyam Maheshwari entered, his eyes cast downward in a sign of respect. "Namaste Dada. I am Shyam Maheshwari." Shyam said, greeting the politician with bowed hands and bent low to touch Shubodh Da's feet.

Shubodh Da gestured for Shyam to take a seat.

"Yes, Shyam. I heard of your troubles. The girls family have threatened to make a police case. If you are charged under this POSCO law and all that? You will be ruined " Shubodh Da was sizing Shyam with small talk, throwing the dreaded POSCO at him.

Shyam literally shuddered at the very thought. Death would be the only answer if such a situation ever came to be.

"I will get you out of it. Don't worry about anything." Shubodh Da told Shyam.

Then he looked at the other man – almost as if in reassurance – "I will handle it. You will not hear a pip squeak from the girl her mother or anyone else with regards to this matter."

There was this pregnant silence. The matter was closed. What's next? Who would speak next?

"Dada, what should be done?" The man asked Shubodh Da.

"No nothing. I don't want any money in this matter." He said.

Then he looked at Shyam Maheshwari and told him, "Whatever you have decided between my man here and yourself that you honour. I don't want any money from you."

Shyam's eyes lit up with curiosity. "How can I thank you Dada?"

"No no – you don't understand. I told you I don't want any money. But I want you to do something else for me." Shubodh Da told Shyam.

"Of course, sir. What do you need me to do?" To be the subservient vassal wasn't a lesson that Shyam Maheshwari needed. That was who he was and that was how he'd climbed the organizational ladder.

Shubodh leaned forward, his voice taking on a conspiratorial tone. "I want you to help me with something. I need you to take care of Helen. You know, the woman my son is seeing? She is working in the same company as you are na?"

Shyam was stunned. He nodded affirmatively. "Yes Sir – she is my colleague. What do you want me to do?"

"For now – you do nothing. You just keep an eye on her. Every couple of days you call me and tell me what happened. Did you see Rohit. Just keep tabs on her. Is she seeing other men? Tell me about her history. I want you to keep a real close eye on her and I want you to understand – this is no ordinary job. You are now working for me. This is your payback to me. I will take care of your problem like it never happened. Happy?" Shubodh Da asked Shyam almost like a benign father talking to his son who'd just landed up in some controversy.

Shyam nodded, understanding. "Yes sir. I don't have to worry about that other matter na?"

Shubodh's expression turned cold. "Yes. When I tell you something once, you don't ask me to repeat myself. I only make promises I can keep. I don't threaten people. I don't make false promises." Shyam winced at the tone and the response. His eyes widened slightly, but he said nothing.

Shyam swallowed hard, knowing that he was getting in deep. But he also knew that he couldn't refuse Shubodh Das Gupta. Not if he wanted to keep his job and his reputation intact.

"Consider it done, sir," Shyam said, his voice barely above a whisper.

Shubodh's eyes gleamed with satisfaction. "Excellent. I knew I could count on you, Shyam."

He looked at the man who brought to him Shyam Maheshwari. "You close your deal with this gentleman. Take whatever was promised to you. Your job is done. From there on – I will deal with this personally. You just ensure that he keeps his end of the bargain. Later in the day, perhaps by this evening, bring that mother and daughter to me. I will settle her problem."

The man was overjoyed. His "To Do Task" for the day was completed. He'd even ask Shyam for a bonus!

And with that, the plan was set in motion. A plan that would change Helen's life forever.

❑❑❑

Chapter 11: The Unraveling

The sun dipped low on the horizon, casting long shadows across the hotel grounds as Senior Police Inspector Pratap Rao Singh sat in the conference room, reviewing the statements gathered from the employees. The tension in the air was palpable, thick with unspoken fears and unresolved suspicions. Aniruddh Pant's nervous confession played on a loop in Pratap's mind, but something about it felt too convenient, too rehearsed.

Pratap's instincts, honed over years of dealing with criminals and corporate sharks alike, told him that there was more to this story than a simple affair gone wrong. Helen's murder had all the hallmarks of a meticulously planned execution, not a crime of passion.

As he pored over the details, a small, seemingly insignificant clue caught his eye—Helen's skin turning a specific shade of blue. While it was an indicator of poisoning, the hue suggested something more sophisticated than the usual suspects like cyanide. He needed answers, and he knew exactly where to get them.

Pratap stood up, his chair scraping loudly against the floor, and strode out of the room. His destination: the hotel bar, where Shyam Maheshwari was known to spend his evenings. The man had been oddly evasive during the initial rounds of questioning, and Pratap was determined to pry open whatever secrets he was hiding.

As Pratap entered the dimly lit bar, the smell of whiskey and stale smoke assaulted his senses. He spotted Shyam sitting in a shadowy corner, nursing a glass of whiskey. The man's eyes flicked up nervously as the inspector approached.

"Mind if I join you?" Pratap's tone left no room for refusal.

Shyam nodded, his hands tightening around the glass. "I already told you everything I know, Inspector."

Pratap sat down, his gaze never leaving Shyam's face. "I believe you, but there's something bothering me. Helen's death—it wasn't just a random act. It was planned, calculated. And you, Shyam, seem to know more than you're letting on."

Shyam's face paled, but he tried to play it off. "I don't know what you mean."

Pratap leaned in closer, lowering his voice. "You see, I've been in this game long enough to know when someone's hiding something. And I can sense that you're scared—not just of the police, but of something, or someone else."

Shyam's eyes darted around the room as if looking for a way out. He swallowed hard and finally spoke, his voice a shaky whisper. "It's not just me, Inspector. There are others... powerful people. People who don't want the truth to come out."

Pratap's interest was piqued. "Go on."

Shyam hesitated, glancing around nervously as if someone might overhear. "The General Manager—Aniruddh Pant—he's not the only one with secrets." He kept on telling "Helen... she was becoming a problem for them. She knew too much."

Pratap leaned back slightly, feigning a casual demeanour to keep Shyam talking. "What did she know?"

Shyam looked around again, his paranoia increasing by the second. "She found out about the dirty dealings. Money laundering, bribes, shady contracts... She thought she could use that information to her advantage, maybe get a promotion, or even blackmail them for more money. But she probably underestimated that it would land her in problems. "

Pratap's eyes narrowed as he absorbed Shyam's words. "And you? What's your role in all of this?"

Shyam let out a hollow laugh, more of a bitter sigh. "I'm just a small cog in the machine. They use me to keep an eye on things, make sure no one steps out of line. But Helen... She was out of my league. I didn't even have the guts to approach her, let alone control her. When she started poking around, I knew it was only a matter of time before something happened."

"Who exactly are 'they'?" Pratap pressed. "Give me names."

Shyam shook his head, his expression one of resigned fear. "I can't... I can't. "

Pratap's patience thinned. He leaned in, his voice a low, dangerous growl. "Listen to me, Shyam. You're already in deep. If you keep holding back, I won't be able to protect you. But if you help me, I might be able to keep you safe. Now, who's behind this?"

Shyam swallowed, beads of sweat forming on his forehead. He looked around one more time, then leaned in closer to Pratap, his voice barely a whisper.

Pratap's mind raced as Shyam's words sank in.

Pratap finished his drink and stood up, his eyes locking onto Shyam's. "Stay low, keep your mouth shut, and don't do anything stupid. I'll be in touch."

Shyam nodded, relief flooding his features as Pratap turned and walked out of the bar. But as Pratap left, he couldn't shake the feeling that Shyam was only telling him part of the story.

"But Shyam, your daughter requires a bone marrow transplant. Isn't it? And you required 1 crore rupees to get treatment in John Hopkins Hospital in USA?" Pratap was very straight this time.

"Yess.., but how did you know?" Shyam started stuttering after a long pause.

"You tried to negotiate a price with a new vendor and Helen heard the conversations. I got to know this from the grapevine. Right?"

Back at his office, Pratap's mind was already working on his next steps. He needed to get to Aniruddh Pant again, but this time, he would press harder. The General Manager knew more than he was letting on, and Pratap was determined to squeeze every bit of information out of him.

The next morning, Pratap strode into the company's headquarters with a purpose. The receptionist's polite smile faltered as she recognized him, and whispers followed him as he made his way to Aniruddh Pant's office.

Aniruddh looked like he hadn't slept in days. His normally crisp suit was wrinkled, and his eyes were bloodshot. He jumped when Pratap entered the room without knocking.

"Inspector," Aniruddh stammered, trying to compose himself. "I wasn't expecting you."

Pratap closed the door behind him, the sound of the latch clicking into place echoing ominously in the room. He walked slowly toward Aniruddh, his eyes never leaving the man's face. "I'm sure you weren't, Mr. Pant. But we need to talk."

Aniruddh fidgeted in his seat, his hands nervously smoothing the creases in his trousers. "I've already told you everything, Inspector. There's nothing more to say."

Pratap stopped in front of the desk, towering over Aniruddh. His voice was calm, but his words carried weight. "I don't think that's true. You see, I've been talking to people—people who seem to think you know a lot more than you're letting on. And I've been doing some digging of my own. Helen was involved in something big, something dangerous. And you're in the middle of it."

Aniruddh's face drained of colour. "I... I don't know what you're talking about."

Pratap leaned in, his voice dropping to a whisper. "You're in over your head, Aniruddh. They had the dirty money, the contracts... Helen found out, didn't she? And now she's dead."

Aniruddh's hands shook as he struggled to maintain his composure. "I didn't kill her. I swear, Inspector. I didn't—"

"I believe you," Pratap interrupted, his voice cold and hard. "But that doesn't mean you're innocent. You knew what was happening, and you did nothing to stop it. You're just as guilty."

Aniruddh's eyes filled with tears, his carefully constructed facade crumbling. "I had no choice... They control everything. If I had tried to stop, I would have been killed by now. You don't understand, Inspector. These people... They're monsters."

Pratap straightened, his eyes boring into Aniruddh's. "Then help me take them down. Give me something I can use—names, evidence, anything."

Aniruddh hesitated, his mind racing. Finally, he nodded, defeated. "There's a file... on my computer. It has everything—the contracts, the payments, the people involved. But you have to promise me protection, Inspector. If I am caught, I'm as good as dead."

Pratap nodded. "I'll do what I can. But you need to cooperate fully. No more lies, no more secrets."

Aniruddh wiped his eyes and unlocked his computer, pulling up the file.

"Sir, it's not opening. I think the file is corrupted."

"Corrupted?? Or you just ensured that the information is no more shareable." Pratap reacted with a stern voice.

"I swear Sir." Aniruddh seems in fix.

As soon as Pratap left, Aniruddh downloaded the file on a USB and deleted the data.

Meanwhile, Pratap's phone buzzed in his pocket, while he was leaving the premises.

It was his forensic expert. He stepped outside Aniruddh's office to take the call.

"Inspector, we've identified the poison," the expert said. "It's Inland Taipan—a rare and highly deadly snake venom substance. It's nearly impossible to trace, but we found traces in Helen's system. This wasn't an accident, Pratap. It was deliberate, and it was planned by someone who knew exactly what they were doing. A rare venom sometimes used in medical research is always smuggled across borders. Also she was pregnant and there was a small prick of needle on her index finger."

Pratap's heart raced as he absorbed the news. Inland Taipan was no ordinary poison. It was the weapon of choice for professionals—people who wanted to kill without leaving a trace. This confirmed his worst suspicions. Helen's murder was a calculated act by someone with the resources and the connections to get away with it.

As Pratap re-entered Aniruddh's office, he knew he was walking into dangerous territory. He couldn't afford to make any mistakes.

"Let's go," Pratap said to Aniruddh, his voice firm. "We're taking this to the station. I'll keep you safe, but you need to stay with me."

Aniruddh nodded, his fear palpable. Together, they left the office, unaware of the shadowy figure watching them from the hallway, a phone pressed to their ear.

The game was far from over. It was only just beginning.

❑❑❑

Chapter 12: A Hidden Agenda

Meanwhile, in the dimly lit corners of the hotel's bar, Pandey Ji nursed his drink, his thoughts racing. The Inspector's questioning had shaken him, and for good reason. He had been privy to many secrets in his long tenure with the company, secrets that were never meant to see the light of day. But this… this was different. Helen's death was not just about corporate rivalry or an affair; it was a message, and Pandey Ji knew exactly who was behind it.

He swirled the amber liquid in his glass, his mind replaying the last few days. He had seen Helen around the hotel, always with that air of quiet confidence, always observing, always listening. She was more than just an employee; she was a threat, one that had been dealt with most permanently. But why? What had she uncovered that warranted such a drastic response?

A hand on his shoulder jolted him out of his thoughts. It was Shyam Maheshwari, the purchase manager, his face a mask of concern. "Pandey Ji, you need to be careful. The police are digging deeper than we thought. If they find out about…"

"Shh!" Pandey Ji cut him off, his voice a harsh whisper.

"Don't mention that here. We'll talk later, in private." But the look in Shyam's eyes told Pandey Ji that time was running out. The game they had played for years was on the verge of unravelling, and the stakes had never been higher.

The two men exchanged a glance, an unspoken understanding passing between them. They had both been in the game long enough to know that loose ends needed to be tied up quickly and quietly. The bar was no place for this discussion.

"Meet me in my office in ten minutes," Pandey Ji muttered, his eyes scanning the room for any prying ears. Shyam nodded curtly and slipped away, leaving Pandey Ji to finish his drink and gather his thoughts.

As he sat there, Pandey Ji couldn't shake the feeling that they were being watched. The shadows seemed to grow longer, and darker, as if they were closing in around him. He had always prided himself on being careful, on staying one step ahead of everyone else. But this time, things were different. The Inspector was digging, and Pandey Ji knew that if they weren't careful, everything they had built could come crashing down.

He tossed back the last of his drink, the alcohol burning a path down his throat, and stood up. It was time to put an end to this once and for all.

Pandey Ji's office was tucked away in a quiet corner of the hotel, far from the bustling activity of the lobby and guest rooms. It was a modest space, but it served its purpose well—privacy. The walls were lined with shelves stacked with files and folders, the remnants of decades of secrets and deals that had kept the company running smoothly. But tonight, those secrets felt like a noose tightening around his neck.

Shyam Maheshwari was already there when Pandey Ji arrived, pacing the small room with nervous energy. The man was a bundle of nerves, his usually slick demeanour cracking under the pressure. He stopped pacing as soon as Pandey Ji entered, his eyes wide with fear.

"They're going to find out, Pandey Ji," Shyam blurted out, his voice trembling. "The Inspector is too close. If he keeps digging…"

Pandey Ji held up a hand to silence him. "Calm down, Shyam. Panicking won't help us. We've dealt with worse situations before."

Shyam shook his head, his hands clenching into fists. "Not like this. Helen was different. She knew things, things she wasn't supposed to know. And now she's dead."

Pandey Ji walked over to his desk, his movements slow and deliberate. He pulled out a chair and sat down, steepling his fingers as he regarded Shyam with a calculating gaze. "What exactly did Helen know, Shyam? You were closer to her than I was."

Pandey Ji's expression hardened. "So, you're telling me that she was going to blow the whistle on all the probable suspects? And now she's dead. Convenient, isn't it?"

Shyam looked up, his eyes pleading. "I didn't kill her, Pandey Ji. I swear. I didn't have the guts. But someone did, and now we're all in danger."

Pandey Ji leaned back in his chair, his mind racing. Shyam was right—Helen's death was too convenient, too well-timed. But who could have done it? Who had the most to lose if Helen had exposed their secrets?

Pandey Ji stood up and walked over to one of the shelves, pulling down a thick file. He opened it and began leafing through the pages, his eyes scanning the contents with practised efficiency. "We have records, transactions, contracts… Everything we've done over the years. But someone has always been careful, keeping his name out of the dirty work. We need something more direct."

Shyam watched anxiously as Pandey Ji continued to search through the file. "Do you think there's something in there?"

Pandey Ji didn't answer immediately, his focus entirely on the documents in front of him. Finally, he stopped on a page and smiled grimly. "Here it is. A transfer they made a few months ago, large enough to raise eyebrows. It was funnelled through several shell companies, but I recognize the pattern. This is our leverage."

Shyam moved closer, peering over Pandey Ji's shoulder. "Is it enough?"

Pandey Ji nodded, his expression resolute. "It has to be. We'll use this to negotiate, to buy our silence. If they know we have this, they'll have no choice but to protect us."

Shyam let out a shaky breath, relief washing over him. "What's the next step?"

Pandey Ji closed the file and placed it back on the shelf. "We need to secure this information, make sure it's safe. And then we wait. The Inspector is going to come after us eventually. When he does, we'll be ready."

Shyam hesitated, his brow furrowing in concern. "And if he finds out about the accounts before we're ready?"

Pandey Ji's eyes turned cold. "Then we take matters into our own hands. We've come too far to let everything fall apart now. We'll do whatever it takes to survive, Shyam. Whatever it takes."

As the night wore on, the two men worked in silence, preparing for the storm they knew was coming. They secured the documents, encrypted the files, and made contingency plans. Every move was calculated, and every decision weighed against the potential fallout. They knew they were walking a fine line, but there was no turning back now.

In the dim light of the office, Pandey Ji glanced at Shyam, who was hunched over his laptop, typing furiously. The man was scared, but he was also loyal. Pandey Ji had seen many men crumble under pressure, but Shyam had always stood by him, no matter how dangerous the situation. They were in this together, and they would get through it together—if they played their cards right.

The following morning, Pandey Ji received a call from the Inspector. Pratap Rao Singh's voice was calm, but Pandey Ji could hear the underlying intensity. The Inspector was closing in, and he wanted to meet again.

"We need to talk, Pandey Ji," Pratap said, his tone leaving no room for refusal. "There are some things that need clarification."

Pandey Ji's heart skipped a beat, but he forced himself to stay calm. "Of course, Inspector. I'll meet you at your office."

"No," Pratap replied sharply. "Let's meet somewhere more private. How about the old warehouse near the docks?"

Pandey Ji hesitated, his mind racing. The warehouse was a secluded location, far from prying eyes. It was the kind of place where deals were made, and secrets were buried. But it was also the kind of place where things could go terribly wrong.

"Very well," Pandey Ji agreed reluctantly. "I'll be there."

As he hung up the phone, Shyam looked up from his laptop, his face pale. "What did he want?"

Pandey Ji rubbed his temples, trying to ease the tension building in his head. "He wants to meet. At the warehouse."

Shyam's eyes widened in alarm. "The warehouse? That's… Why there? It's too risky."

Pandey Ji nodded, his thoughts echoing Shyam's concerns. "I know. But we don't have a choice. If we refuse, it'll only make us look guilty. We have to play along, see what he knows."

Shyam swallowed hard, his fingers trembling as he reached for a cigarette. "What if it's a trap?"

Pandey Ji sighed, watching as Shyam lit the cigarette and took a shaky drag. "It might be. But we'll be prepared. We're not walking into this blind."

The two men exchanged a tense glance, the gravity of the situation settling heavily between them. They were walking into a lion's den, and they both knew it. But they also knew that they had no choice. The only way out was through.

Later that day, as the sun began to set, Pandey Ji and Shyam Maheshwari drove to the warehouse. The streets were empty, the shadows long and ominous. The city felt different, quieter, as if it was holding its breath, waiting for something to happen.

When they arrived at the warehouse, they found Pratap already there, leaning against his car with a cigarette in hand. His eyes were sharp, watching their every move as they stepped out of the vehicle.

"Inspector," Pandey Ji greeted him with a nod, keeping his voice neutral. "What's this about?"

Pratap took a slow drag of his cigarette before flicking it to the ground and crushing it under his boot. "I've been doing some digging, Pandey Ji. Found some interesting things about the company's finances. Offshore accounts, shell companies, and money disappear without a trace. Care to explain?"

Pandey Ji's heart pounded in his chest, but he kept his expression calm. "I don't know what you're talking about, Inspector. We run a clean operation."

Pratap's eyes narrowed, his gaze piercing. "Don't play games with me, Pandey Ji. You and I both know that's not true. Helen found out, didn't she? And now she's dead."

Pandey Ji clenched his fists, his mind racing for a response. "You have no proof."

Pratap smirked, his eyes gleaming with determination. "Not yet. But I will. And when I do, you're going down."

The tension in the air was thick, the warehouse silent except for the sound of their breathing. Pandey Ji knew he was cornered, but he wasn't going to go down without a fight.

"We'll see about that, Inspector," Pandey Ji replied, his voice steady despite the turmoil inside him. "But until then, you should watch your back. You're playing a dangerous game."

Pratap's smile faded, his expression turning serious. "So are you, Pandey Ji. So are you."

The two men stared each other down, the weight of their unspoken threats hanging heavy in the air. Shyam shifted nervously beside Pandey Ji, his fingers twitching at his side.

He could feel the danger, the potential for violence simmering just beneath the surface.

Finally, Pratap broke the silence. "This isn't over. Not by a long shot. I'll be watching you, Pandey Ji. Every move you make."

With that, the Inspector turned and walked back to his car, leaving Pandey Ji and Shyam standing in the fading light, the weight of his words settling heavily on their shoulders.

As they watched Pratap's car disappear into the distance, Shyam let out a shaky breath. "What now?"

Pandey Ji stared after the car, his mind already racing with possibilities. "Now? Now we prepare for war."

❑❑❑

Chapter 13: Pratap's Revelation

Pratap Rao Singh returned to his office late that evening, his mind still reeling from the tense encounter at the warehouse. The sun had long since set, leaving the city shrouded in darkness, and the streets outside his window were eerily quiet. But inside his mind, the wheels were still turning, relentlessly piecing together the fragments of the case.

As he entered his office, the soft glow of his desk lamp illuminated a stack of papers that had been neatly arranged by his assistant. Among them was a large manila envelope, marked with the bold red lettering of the forensic department. Pratap's pulse quickened as he tore open the envelope, eager to see what new information awaited him.

The report was concise, yet chilling. The poison used to kill Helen was identified as Inland Taipan, a rare and deadly snake venom. Pratap's eyes scanned the report, absorbing the details. Inland Taipan was known for causing an instant and agonizing death, one that paralyzed its victims while leaving them fully conscious. Moreover tracing is extremely difficult as testing tools are not designed for such deadly venom.

Pratap leaned back in his chair, staring at the ceiling as the implications sank in. This was no ordinary crime. Whoever had killed Helen had gone to great lengths to ensure her death was both excruciating and untraceable. The use of such a rare toxin pointed to someone with connections—someone who knew exactly what they were doing.

But why? What had Helen done to deserve such a fate? The question gnawed at him, refusing to let go.

He picked up the phone and dialed a number from memory. It rang only once before a gruff voice answered. "Goa Police, Inspector Malik speaking."

"Malik, it's Pratap. I need a favor."

There was a pause on the other end, followed by a chuckle. "Pratap Rao Singh, as I live and breathe. What brings the great inspector to my humble domain?"

Pratap smiled faintly at the familiar banter. "I need some information about a family in your area. The D'Souzas. Specifically, Helen D'Souza."

The line went quiet for a moment, and Pratap could hear the rustling of papers in the background. "Helen D'Souza, you say? That name rings a bell. What's this about, Pratap?"

"She's dead. Murdered. And I have reason to believe her past might hold the key to why."

Malik's tone shifted, becoming more serious. "I see. Give me a moment."

Pratap waited as Malik typed away at his computer, the faint sound of keys clicking echoing through the line. After a few minutes, Malik spoke again.

"Pratap, you're not going to like what I found. Helen's father, Peter D'Souza, was deeply involved in the local fishing industry—specifically, the illicit trade of exotic marine life. He had a reputation for being ruthless, willing to do whatever it took to stay on top. There were rumors that he dabbled in smuggling pufferfish for the black market, among other things."

Pratap felt a chill run down his spine. The dots started to connect in his mind, forming a dark and twisted picture. Had Helen stumbled upon something she wasn't supposed to? Or worse, had she been involved in it?

"Is Peter D'Souza still around?" Pratap asked, his voice tense.

"No," Malik replied. "He died a few years ago—car accident, if I recall correctly. But the business didn't die with him. His associates kept it going, and from what I hear, his daughter was involved. Helen wasn't just some innocent bystander, Pratap. She knew what she was doing."

Pratap's grip tightened on the phone. "Do you have any contacts who might know more?"

"I can make some calls," Malik offered. "But be careful, Pratap. These people don't take kindly to outsiders poking around in their affairs."

"Thanks, Malik. I owe you one."

"Just stay alive long enough to repay the favor," Malik quipped before hanging up.

Pratap sat in silence for a moment, his mind racing. Helen's connection to the illicit trade of exotic marine life changed everything. This wasn't just about corporate rivalry or blackmail—it was about something far more dangerous. And if Helen had been involved, it was no wonder she had ended up dead.

But who had killed her? Was it one of her father's old associates, trying to silence her before she could expose them? Or was it someone within the company, desperate to keep their own secrets buried? Can it be Shyam, for her daughter? Can it be the Research and development head, who was always insecure of losing his job? Even Helen wanted some good amount of money by selling company information. Was the poison meant for someone else and Helen died of an accident.

Almost everyone is a suspect here.

Pratap knew he needed to dig deeper, to uncover the full extent of Helen's involvement. He pulled up her personnel file on his computer, scanning through the details with a critical eye. There were no obvious red flags, but Pratap had learned long ago that the most dangerous people were often the ones who blended in the best.

He made a list of names—people Helen had interacted with both inside and outside of work. Her colleagues, her friends, her family. There were too many loose ends, too many questions left unanswered.

As he pored over the details, one name kept coming up: Rajiv Menon. He was a quiet, unassuming man, but he had been close to Helen. Too close, perhaps. Pratap remembered seeing Rajiv at the hotel, always lingering on the periphery, watching but never speaking. There was something about him that didn't sit right with Pratap.

He picked up the phone again and dialed Rajiv's number. It rang several times before a voice answered, shaky and uncertain.

"Hello?"

"Rajiv, it's Inspector Pratap Rao Singh. We need to talk."

There was a pause, and Pratap could hear Rajiv's breathing quicken on the other end of the line. "Is this about Helen?"

"Yes," Pratap replied bluntly. "I have some questions, and I'd prefer to ask them in person. Can you meet me at the station?"

"I… I don't know if that's a good idea," Rajiv stammered. "I don't want to get involved in all this."

"You're already involved, Rajiv," Pratap said, his voice firm. "Whether you like it or not. Now, are you coming in voluntarily, or do I need to send someone to bring you in?"

There was a long silence, followed by a resigned sigh. "Alright. I'll be there in an hour."

Pratap hung up the phone, his thoughts swirling. Rajiv knew something—he was sure of it. And if he could get the man to talk, he might finally get the answers he needed.

An hour later, Rajiv Menon sat across from Pratap in the interrogation room, his hands trembling as he clutched a cup of coffee. His eyes darted around the room, avoiding Pratap's gaze.

"Relax, Rajiv," Pratap said, trying to put the man at ease. "I'm not here to accuse you of anything. I just need to understand what happened."

Rajiv nodded shakily, taking a sip of his coffee. "I… I don't know much. Helen and I… we were friends, but we didn't talk about work."

"But you knew about her family," Pratap pressed. "About her father's business."

Rajiv's eyes widened, and he nearly dropped his cup. "How… How did you…?"

"That doesn't matter," Pratap interrupted. "What matters is that you knew. And I need to know what Helen was involved in. Was she still connected to her father's old associates?"

Rajiv hesitated, glancing down at his hands. "I don't know for sure. She never talked about it, not directly. But… there were things. She'd get these phone calls, late at night. And sometimes she'd disappear for a day or two, no explanation. I asked her about it once, but she just brushed me off."

Pratap leaned forward, his voice low and intense. "Did she ever mention any names? Anyone she was worried about?"

Rajiv shook his head. "No, but… there was one thing. A few weeks before she died, she told me she was scared. She didn't say why, but I could tell something was wrong. She was looking over her shoulder all the time, like she was being watched."

Pratap's mind raced. Helen had known she was in danger, but she hadn't told anyone. Why? Was she trying to protect someone, or had she been planning something of her own?

"Rajiv, I need you to think carefully," Pratap said, his tone serious. "Is there anything else you can tell me? Anything at all?"

Rajiv hesitated again, then slowly nodded. "There was one more thing. I found this… this notebook in her apartment after she died. It was hidden under a floorboard. I didn't know what to do with it, so I kept it."

Pratap's heart skipped a beat. "Do you still have it?"

Rajiv nodded. "Yes. I… I can bring it to you."

"Do that," Pratap said, his voice firm. "And Rajiv… if you're holding anything else back, now's the time to tell me."

Rajiv shook his head frantically. "No, that's it. I swear."

"Good. Bring me the notebook, and we'll go from there."

Certainly! I'll pick up from where the story left off and continue the scene with Rajiv. I'll also ensure the chapter reaches its conclusion with a strong finish.

The next morning, Rajiv arrived at the station, clutching a small, worn notebook in his hands. His knuckles were white from the pressure, and his eyes darted around nervously as he entered Pratap's office. He handed the notebook to Pratap, his hands trembling.

"This is it," Rajiv whispered, as if afraid someone might overhear. "This is all I have."

Pratap took the notebook, his fingers brushing over the worn cover. It felt heavy in his hands, not just in weight but in significance. This little book could be the key to unlocking the mystery behind Helen's death.

"Thank you, Rajiv," Pratap said, his voice calm and measured. "You've done the right thing."

Rajiv nodded, but his face remained pale. "I hope so, Inspector. I just want this nightmare to be over."

Pratap watched as Rajiv left the office, his footsteps echoing down the hall. The man was clearly shaken, and Pratap couldn't blame him. He knew that getting involved in something like this was dangerous, and Rajiv had taken a big risk by coming forward.

Once he was alone, Pratap carefully opened the notebook. The pages were filled with Helen's neat, precise handwriting. At first glance, it appeared to be a simple journal, but as Pratap flipped through the pages, he began to see the patterns emerge.

Helen had been meticulous in her documentation. She had kept records of phone calls, meetings, and transactions—all of it coded, but the meaning was clear to Pratap. She had been gathering evidence against her father's old associates, tracking their illegal activities and compiling enough information to bring them down. But somewhere along the way, she had become entangled in their web. Perhaps she had underestimated just how dangerous they were.

One page, in particular, caught Pratap's attention. It was a list of names—people Helen had been in contact with. Some of the names were familiar: Shyam Maheshwari, Aniruddh Pant, even some of the hotel staff. But others were less so, marked only by initials and vague references. At the bottom of the list, a single word was underlined: "O".

Pratap's pulse quickened. Helen had been investigating the very people who controlled the company, and it had cost her her life. But the question remained: who had silenced her? Was it the owners themselves, or had someone else taken matters into their own hands?

As he continued reading, another revelation struck him. Helen had known about the Inland Taipan. One of her last entries mentioned it by name, along with a contact in the black market who could procure it. It wasn't just an accident—she had been preparing for something, perhaps even planning to use the venom herself. But instead, it had been used against her.

Pratap's mind raced. The pieces were starting to come together, but there were still gaps. He needed to know more about these owners and their connection to the illicit trade. Helen's father had been involved in. And he needed to find out who else had access to the Inland Taipan.

He picked up the phone and dialed Malik again. The line connected, and Malik's voice came through, sounding groggy.

"Pratap? It's early, man. What's going on?"

"Malik, I need another favor," Pratap said, his voice urgent. "I need you to dig deeper into Peter D'Souza's old associates. Specifically, anyone who might have connections to the black market and exotic snake venom like Inland Taipan."

Malik let out a low whistle. "You're not messing around, are you? Alright, give me a few hours. I'll see what I can find."

Pratap thanked him and hung up, his mind already shifting to the next steps. He had to confront the owners—there was no way around it. But he couldn't do it blindly. He needed more leverage, more proof.

The day wore on as Pratap delved deeper into Helen's notes. He cross-referenced the information with what he already knew, trying to build a complete picture of the web of deceit that had ensnared her. The more he uncovered, the more dangerous it all seemed. And yet, Pratap couldn't shake the feeling that he was still missing something—something crucial.

As the sun began to set, casting long shadows across his office, Pratap's phone rang again. It was Malik.

"I've got something for you," Malik said, his voice tense. "There's a name that keeps coming up in connection with Peter D'Souza's old operations. A guy named Raghav. He's been off the radar for a while, but he was one of Peter's top enforcers back in the day. If anyone knows about the toxin or the connections to the owners, it's him."

Pratap's grip tightened on the phone. "Where can I find him?"

"Last I heard, he was laying low in a little village on the outskirts of Goa. But be careful, Pratap. This guy is bad news. If he thinks you're onto him, he won't hesitate to take you out."

Pratap nodded, though Malik couldn't see him. "Thanks, Malik. I'll be careful."

He hung up and leaned back in his chair, his mind racing with possibilities. Raghav could be the key to everything, but tracking him down would be risky. Still, Pratap knew he had no choice. He had come too far to turn back now.

The next morning, Pratap packed a small bag and made

arrangements for a flight to Goa. He left instructions with his team, ensuring that the investigation would continue in his absence. But he didn't tell them the full extent of his plan. This was something he had to handle alone.

As the plane soared through the clouds, Pratap stared out the window, his mind replaying everything he had learned so far. Helen's death, the Inland Taipan, her father's dark legacy—it all pointed to a conspiracy that ran deeper than he had imagined. But he was determined to see it through, no matter the cost.

When he arrived in Goa, the heat and humidity hit him like a wave. The vibrant colors and bustling streets were a stark contrast to the dark thoughts swirling in his mind. He hailed a taxi and gave the driver directions to the village where Raghav was rumored to be hiding.

The journey was long, the roads winding through dense forests and small villages. As they neared their destination, Pratap felt a knot of tension tighten in his chest. This was it—the moment of truth.

The village was small and unassuming, nestled between the hills and the sea. Pratap paid the driver and stepped out, his eyes scanning the area. He didn't know what Raghav looked like, but he had a feeling the man would stand out in a place like this.

He approached a local vendor, showing him a picture he had managed to dig up from the old police archives. The man squinted at the photo, then nodded slowly.

"Raghav? He lives down by the old pier. But be careful—he's not someone you want to mess with."

Pratap thanked the man and made his way to the pier. The smell of saltwater and decaying fish filled the air, and the sound of waves crashing against the rocks provided a haunting backdrop. As he approached a small, weathered house at the edge of the pier, Pratap's hand instinctively moved to the gun holstered at his side.

He knocked on the door, his senses on high alert. After a few moments, the door creaked open, revealing a tall, muscular man with cold, calculating eyes. This had to be Raghav.

"What do you want?" Raghav's voice was rough, like gravel.

"Inspector Pratap Rao Singh," Pratap said, holding up his badge. "I have some questions for you."

Raghav's eyes flicked to the badge, then back to Pratap's face. He smirked. "I don't talk to cops."

"This isn't a request," Pratap replied, his voice firm. "It's about Helen D'Souza."

At the mention of Helen's name, Raghav's expression darkened. He stepped aside, gesturing for Pratap to enter. The inside of the house was sparse, with little more than a table, a few chairs, and a bed. The air was thick with tension.

"You've got five minutes," Raghav said, crossing his arms.

Pratap wasted no time. "Helen was killed with Inland Taipan. A rare poison, not something you can just pick up at the local market. I know you were close to her father, and I know you have connections in the black market. What do you know about the toxin, and who gave it to her?"

Raghav's eyes narrowed, but he didn't respond immediately. Pratap could see the wheels turning in the man's mind, calculating whether it was worth telling the truth.

Finally, Raghav spoke, his voice low and dangerous. "I don't know who gave her the toxin. But I can tell you this—Helen was playing a dangerous game. She thought she could use what she knew to get ahead, to get out. But she was in way over her head."

"Who was she trying to get out from under?" Pratap pressed.

Raghav hesitated, then shook his head. "You're asking the wrong questions, Inspector. It's not about who—it's about what. She was trying to take down the whole operation, bring it crashing down. But she didn't realize how deep it went, how many people were involved."

Pratap's heart raced. "Are you saying the owners were behind it?"

Raghav let out a bitter laugh. "The owners? They're just the tip of the iceberg. This goes way beyond them, way beyond anything you can imagine."

Pratap's mind reeled. The conspiracy was bigger than he had anticipated, and the danger more immediate. But he wasn't about to back down now.

"Then help me," Pratap said, his voice steady. "Help me bring them down."

Raghav's eyes locked onto Pratap's, and for a moment, the tension in the room was palpable. Then, slowly, Raghav nodded.

"I'll help you, Inspector. But understand this—once we start, there's no turning back. You're in this for the long haul."

Pratap nodded, determination etched into his features. "I understand. Let's end this."

As they began to plan their next move, Pratap couldn't shake the feeling that they were on the edge of something monumental. The truth was within reach, but so was the danger. And as they prepared to take down the powerful forces behind Helen's death, Pratap knew that the real battle was only just beginning.

❑❑❑

Chapter 14: A Dangerous Alliance

The sun had barely risen when Pratap Rao Singh arrived at the station. His night had been restless, filled with half-formed plans and lingering doubts. The revelation about Helen's connection to the illicit trade had opened up a labyrinth of possibilities, each more dangerous than the last. But the most pressing issue on his mind was the owners—those shadowy figures who controlled everything from behind the scenes.

He had summoned Aniruddh Pant for another round of questioning, determined to pry loose whatever secrets the man was still hiding. When Aniruddh finally walked into the interrogation room, Pratap could sense that something had changed. The General Manager, though still visibly nervous, had a steely resolve in his eyes. He had prepared for this.

Aniruddh sat down across from Pratap, folding his hands on the table. Before Pratap could speak, he cut in.

"I know what you're thinking, Inspector," Aniruddh began, his voice steady. "You think I killed Helen because of our affair, that I was trying to protect my position, my family. But you're wrong. Helen was a threat to someone much more powerful than me."

Pratap leaned back in his chair, intrigued by Aniruddh's sudden willingness to talk. He had expected resistance, but instead, he found a man ready to confess—though not in the way he had anticipated. "Go on," Pratap urged.

Aniruddh sighed deeply, running a hand through his hair as if trying to smooth out his tangled thoughts. "Helen wasn't just climbing the corporate ladder; she was digging into the company's financials, looking for discrepancies. She found something—something big. Offshore accounts, shell companies, all tied to someone higher up. She came to me because she didn't know who else to trust."

Pratap's eyes narrowed, his mind racing. "Who?" he pressed.

Aniruddh hesitated for a moment, then leaned in closer, lowering his voice to a whisper. "The owners," he said. "They've been laundering money through the company for years. Helen found out, and they silenced her before she could go public."

Pratap felt a cold chill run down his spine. This was bigger than he had imagined. If Aniruddh was telling the truth, then Helen's murder was just the tip of the iceberg. But he needed proof, and he knew exactly where to find it.

"I need details, Aniruddh," Pratap said, his voice calm but firm. "Names, dates, transactions—everything you know."

Aniruddh nodded, his expression resolute. "I've been keeping records, just in case. I didn't want to get caught up in their mess, but I knew it was only a matter of time before something like this happened. I have a file hidden in my office, encrypted. It has everything you need."

Pratap raised an eyebrow. "And why haven't you handed this over sooner?"

Aniruddh's gaze faltered for a moment before he answered. "Because I was scared, Inspector. Scared of what they might do to me, to my family. But now… now I realize that keeping quiet isn't going to protect me. If they killed Helen, they won't hesitate to kill me too."

Pratap studied Aniruddh's face, searching for any sign of deception. But the man seemed sincere, his fear palpable. Still, Pratap knew better than to trust anyone completely—not in this game.

"Alright," Pratap said finally. "You're going to get me that file, and in return, I'll do my best to protect you. But understand this, Aniruddh—if you're lying to me, if you're holding anything back, I won't be able to help you when they come for you."

Aniruddh nodded, his face pale but determined. "I understand, Inspector. I'll get you the file."

Pratap stood up, signaling the end of their conversation. "I'll arrange for an officer to escort you back to your office. Make sure you don't try anything foolish."

As Aniruddh was led out of the room, Pratap couldn't shake

the feeling that he was walking into a trap. But he had no choice. If Aniruddh's information was genuine, it could blow the entire case wide open.

An hour later, Pratap arrived at the company's headquarters with Aniruddh in tow. The building loomed ominously above them, its sleek glass façade reflecting the pale morning light. Inside, the atmosphere was tense, with employees casting nervous glances at the Inspector as he walked by. They all knew why he was here, and they all feared what might come next.

Aniruddh led Pratap to his office, his hands trembling slightly as he unlocked the door. The room was just as Pratap remembered—neatly organized, with shelves of files and a sleek computer on the desk. But today, there was an air of unease that hadn't been there before.

Aniruddh moved quickly to his desk, typing in a series of commands on his computer. Pratap watched closely, his hand resting on the gun at his side. He couldn't afford to take any chances.

After a few tense moments, Aniruddh turned the monitor toward Pratap. "Here it is," he said quietly. "The file."

Pratap stepped forward, his eyes scanning the screen. The file was encrypted, just as Aniruddh had said, but it wasn't anything Pratap couldn't handle. He pulled out a USB drive and inserted it into the computer, copying the file with practiced efficiency.

As the progress bar filled, Pratap's mind raced. If this file contained what Aniruddh claimed, it could be the key to bringing down the entire operation. But it also made him a target—one step closer to the crosshairs of whoever had orchestrated Helen's murder.

When the transfer was complete, Pratap removed the USB drive and slipped it into his pocket. "I'll take it from here," he said, his tone leaving no room for argument.

Aniruddh nodded, relief washing over his features. "What happens now, Inspector?"

"Now," Pratap replied, "you go home and stay there. I'll be in touch when I have more information. And remember—keep your mouth shut. The less you say, the safer you'll be."

Aniruddh swallowed hard, but he nodded again. "Understood."

As Pratap left the office, his thoughts were already shifting to his next move. He needed to analyze the file, to see if it held the proof he needed. But more importantly, he needed to figure out who within the company was pulling the strings. The owners were still a shadowy presence, untouchable for now, but if he could connect them to the illicit activities, he would have the leverage he needed to take them down.

Back at the station, Pratap locked himself in his office and plugged the USB drive into his computer. The encryption was strong, but not impenetrable. It took him several hours to crack the code, but when the file finally opened, Pratap's breath caught in his throat.

The file was a goldmine of information. Bank statements, wire transfers, shell companies—it was all there, laid out in meticulous detail. The money had been funneled through various offshore accounts, disguised as legitimate business expenses. But the real shock came when Pratap saw the names attached to the transactions.

The owners were involved, just as Aniruddh had said. But they weren't the only ones. There were other names—high-ranking executives, government officials, even members of the police force. The corruption ran deep, entangling powerful people from all walks of life.

Pratap's hands shook as he scrolled through the data. This wasn't just about Helen anymore. This was about a system of corruption that had been festering for years, hidden behind the glossy exterior of the company. And now, he had the proof to expose it.

But with that proof came a dangerous realization. He was in over his head. The people he was up against wouldn't hesitate to kill to protect their secrets, and now that he had the evidence, he was a threat to all of them.

Pratap knew he needed to act quickly. He couldn't trust anyone, not even his colleagues. The only way to stay ahead was to stay one step ahead of the people who wanted him dead.

He made a series of calls, contacting a few trusted allies who operated outside the official channels. He needed to move the evidence somewhere safe, somewhere it couldn't be tampered with. And he needed to start planning his next move—how to bring this information to light without getting himself killed in the process.

As the night wore on, Pratap's office became a war room, filled with maps, files, and encrypted communications. He worked tirelessly, driven by a sense of urgency that wouldn't let him rest. The clock was ticking, and every second that passed brought him closer to the inevitable confrontation.

He was drawing suspects.

"Maybe Anirudh because he had the motive to hide his illicit affair. But how did he access the poison?

Maybe Shyam because he hated both Anirudh and Helen. But did he have any access to poison?

Maybe Pandey ji because he had access to the poison. But what could be his motive?

Can it be Jeeva Rao because he hated Anirudh and Helen and also had access to the poison?

Maybe Rohit because he may have discovered that Helen was pregnant. But how could he administer the poison?"

Now Pratap had the birthday details of all employees (except Rohit) from the admin records of the company. He had studied their horoscope. And from Palmistry the shape of thumb and fingers of all. Incidentally murderous criminals have a typical thumb and inward bent fingers. Based on the above he narrowed down his list to three - Shyam, Pandey ji and possibly Rohit. Also, whoever was responsible for her pregnancy had a strong motive.

He needed to talk to these 3 again.

The following morning, Pratap received a call from an unexpected source. It was Raghav, the man he had confronted in Goa, and the last person he expected to hear from.

"I hear you've been busy, Inspector," Raghav's voice was calm, but there was an edge to it. "Seems you've stirred up quite the hornet's nest."

Pratap frowned, his mind racing. "What do you want, Raghav?"

"I'm offering you a deal," Raghav replied, his tone as smooth as silk. "You've got information that a lot of people would pay good money to keep buried. But I've got connections, Inspector—connections that could help you stay alive long enough to do something with that information."

Pratap's grip on the phone tightened. He knew better than to trust a man like Raghav, but he also knew that he was running out of options. "What's the catch?"

"No catch," Raghav said, though his voice carried a hint of amusement. "Just mutual interests. You want to bring down the people responsible for Helen's death, and I want to make sure certain... parties don't get too powerful. We can help each other."

Pratap didn't like the sound of this alliance, but he couldn't afford to dismiss it outright. "And what exactly do you propose?"

"Meet me tonight," Raghav said. "I'll send you the location. We'll talk, face to face. You'll get what you need to take them down, and in return, I'll get what I need to keep things balanced."

Pratap hesitated for a moment, weighing his options. He knew that dealing with Raghav was dangerous, but the alternative—going after the owners and their associates without any backup—was even more so. If he wanted to survive this, he needed every advantage he could get.

"Fine," Pratap said finally. "But if you try to double-cross me—"

"I wouldn't dream of it," Raghav interrupted with a chuckle. "See you tonight, Inspector."

The line went dead, leaving Pratap staring at the phone in his hand. He didn't trust Raghav as far as he could throw him, but right now, he didn't have the luxury of being picky. The stakes were too high.

Later that evening, Pratap found himself in a dimly lit warehouse on the outskirts of the city. The place was deserted, save for a few rusting crates and broken machinery scattered around the floor. The only sound was the distant hum of traffic outside.

Raghav emerged from the shadows, his face partially obscured by the brim of his hat. He approached Pratap with an easy confidence, as if he had all the time in the world.

"Inspector," Raghav greeted him with a nod. "I'm glad you came."

"Let's get this over with," Pratap replied, his voice cold. "What do you have for me?"

Raghav reached into his coat and pulled out a small, unmarked envelope. "Inside this envelope, you'll find everything you need to tie the owners directly to the illicit activities Helen was investigating. Bank records, wire transfers, names, dates—it's all there."

Pratap took the envelope, but his eyes remained fixed on Raghav. "And why are you giving me this?"

"Like I said, mutual interests," Raghav replied smoothly. "The owners are getting greedy, expanding their reach. If they're allowed to continue unchecked, they'll upset the balance. And that's bad for business."

Pratap nodded slowly, understanding more than Raghav had said outright. The man was protecting his own turf, ensuring that no one got too powerful. It was a dangerous game, but one that could work in Pratap's favor.

"And what's to stop you from using this against me later?" Pratap asked, his tone cautious.

Raghav smiled faintly. "Let's just say that I've found it's better to have a friend in the police force than an enemy. As long as we keep this... arrangement, I see no reason to turn on you."

Pratap pocketed the envelope, his mind already racing with

how to use the information inside. He didn't trust Raghav, but for now, they were aligned in their goals. And that was enough.

"I'll hold you to that," Pratap said, his voice firm.

Raghav tipped his hat. "I'm sure you will, Inspector. Good luck. You're going to need it."

With that, Raghav melted back into the shadows, leaving Pratap alone in the warehouse. The Inspector stood there for a moment, the weight of the envelope heavy in his pocket. He knew that what he held in his hand was both a weapon and a target. It could bring down powerful people, but it could also get him killed.

Pratap turned and walked out of the warehouse, his mind focused on the next steps. He had the evidence he needed, but now came the hardest part—exposing it without getting caught in the crossfire.

As he drove back to the station, the city lights flickering in the distance, Pratap couldn't shake the feeling that the final act was about to begin. The players were all in place, and the stakes had never been higher. But this time, he was ready.

He would take them down. All of them.

Chapter 15: The Final Gambit

Pandey Ji's heart pounded as he approached the owner's suite. The corridor seemed longer than usual, the walls closing in on him as his footsteps echoed off the polished marble floors. He had been summoned, and he knew that this was no ordinary meeting. The tension in the air was palpable, and Pandey Ji could feel the weight of the impending confrontation pressing down on his shoulders.

The door to the suite opened before he could knock, and he was ushered inside by a man he had never seen before—a tall, imposing figure with cold, calculating eyes that seemed to see right through him. The man's presence alone set off alarm bells in Pandey Ji's mind. This wasn't just another meeting; this was something far more dangerous.

"Sit down, Pandey Ji," the owner's voice came from behind a large, ornate desk that dominated the room."We need to have a talk."

Pandey Ji sat, his hands trembling slightly as he placed them on his lap. He had been in the owner's presence countless times before, but never like this. The air was thick with unspoken threats, and the look in the owner's eyes sent a chill down his spine.

"Sir, I—" Pandey Ji began, but the owner cut him off with a sharp gesture.

Pandey Ji felt a surge of panic rise in his chest. He had known that things were spiraling out of control, but hearing it spelled out so bluntly shook him to the core. He had spent years building his loyalty to the owners, protecting their interests, and ensuring their dirty secrets remained hidden. But now, in this moment, he realized that all of it meant nothing. He was expendable, just like Helen.

"Sir, I didn't—" Pandey Ji started, but the look in the owner's eyes silenced him. The cold, ruthless expression left no room for excuses.

"Your loyalty has been useful, Pandey Ji," the owner continued, his voice calm and measured. "But we can't afford any loose ends. You understand what needs to be done."

Pandey Ji nodded slowly, his mind racing. He knew exactly what the owner meant. The message was clear: either he cleaned up the mess, or he became part of it. The realization hit him like a punch to the gut—his fate was already sealed.

As he left the suite, his legs felt like lead, and the world outside seemed to blur around him. The weight of the situation bore down on him, suffocating him with its intensity. He had always known that his position came with risks, but he had never imagined it would come to this. The owners had used him, and now they were discarding him like a broken tool.

But as Pandey Ji walked down the hallway, a thought began to form in his mind—a desperate, last-ditch plan that might just save him. He knew that if he was going to survive, he couldn't rely on the owners anymore. He had to take matters into his own hands, and perhaps, for once in his life, do the right thing.

Pandey Ji spent the next few hours in his office, the door locked and the blinds drawn. He knew he was being watched—there were eyes and ears everywhere, especially in a place like this. But he had to stay calm, had to think clearly. The plan he was hatching was dangerous, but it was the only chance he had left.

He reached for his phone, dialing a number he hadn't used in years. The line rang twice before a voice answered, gruff and familiar.

"Pandey Ji. It's been a long time."

"Too long," Pandey Ji replied, his voice steady despite the turmoil inside him. "I need a favor."

There was a pause on the other end of the line, and Pandey Ji could almost hear the gears turning in the man's mind. "What kind of favor?"

"The kind that comes with a price," Pandey Ji said, knowing full well what he was asking for. "I need protection. And I need to disappear."

Another pause, longer this time. "You're in deep, aren't you?"

"You could say that," Pandey Ji admitted. "But this isn't just about me. There's something bigger at play, and if I don't act now, a lot of people are going to get hurt."

The voice on the other end let out a low whistle. "Alright, Pandey Ji. I'll see what I can do. But this won't be easy, and it won't be cheap."

"Just tell me where and when," Pandey Ji replied. "I'll handle the rest."

The call ended, and Pandey Ji leaned back in his chair, staring at the ceiling. He had just set the wheels in motion for what would be the most dangerous move of his life. But he knew he had no other choice. The owners had made it clear that he was expendable, and if he didn't act now, he would be dead by the end of the week.

But as he sat there, his mind began to turn to another thought—one that had been gnawing at him ever since the meeting with the owner. Could he really walk away from all of this? Could he leave behind the life he had built, the power and influence he had accumulated over the years? The thought of disappearing, of becoming a nobody, terrified him more than the thought of dying.

And then there was the matter of Helen. Pandey Ji had been complicit in her death, even if he hadn't pulled the trigger. He had known what was happening, and he had done nothing to stop it. The guilt weighed heavily on him, and for the first time in his life, he wondered if there was a way to make things right.

The following day, Pandey Ji made his move. He left the office early, telling his colleagues that he had a meeting outside of the hotel. In reality, he was heading to a storage unit on the outskirts of the city—a place where he had stashed away documents, records, and other items he had kept as insurance over the years. It was his safety net, his way out if things ever went south.

As he entered the dimly lit storage unit, the cold air hit him like a slap in the face. He shivered, but not just from the temperature. This place represented everything he had done, everything he had become. And now, it was the key to his survival.

He began rifling through the boxes, pulling out files and papers that detailed the company's illicit activities. There were records of transactions, names of people involved, and even evidence of bribes paid to law enforcement and government officials. It was all there, laid out in black and white. Enough to bring down the entire operation.

But as Pandey Ji gathered the documents, a new idea began to take shape in his mind. What if he didn't just disappear? What if he used this information to turn the tables on the owners? If he could expose them, he could not only save himself but also bring justice to those who had been hurt by their actions. It was a dangerous gamble, but one that could change everything.

He hesitated for a moment, weighing his options. Disappearing was the safer choice, the one that would guarantee his survival.

But it also meant abandoning everything, running for the rest of his life. Exposing the owners, on the other hand, was risky—one wrong move, and he would be dead. But it also meant redemption, a chance to make things right.

In the end, the decision was made for him. As he was packing up the last of the documents, his phone buzzed with a text message. It was from the man he had called the night before—the one who was supposed to help him disappear.

They know. You need to move now. Meet me at the docks in one hour. Don't be late.

Pandey Ji's heart raced as he read the message. They knew. The owners were on to him, and his time was running out. He had no choice—he had to act now, before it was too late.

An hour later, Pandey Ji stood at the docks, the cold night air biting into his skin. The place was deserted, the only sounds the lapping of the waves against the pier and the distant hum of the city. He clutched the briefcase containing the documents tightly in his hand, his eyes scanning the darkness for any sign of movement.

A car pulled up a few minutes later, its headlights cutting through the fog. The door opened, and the man he had called stepped out. He was tall and broad-shouldered, with a face that was both familiar and threatening.

"Pandey Ji," the man greeted him, his voice low. "You've got what I need?"

Pandey Ji nodded, holding up the briefcase. "It's all here. But I need something from you in return."

The man raised an eyebrow. "And what might that be?"

"Protection," Pandey Ji replied, "and a guarantee that this information will be used to bring down the people responsible for Helen's death—and everything else they've done."

The man eyed the briefcase, his expression unreadable. "That's a tall order, Pandey Ji. You're asking for a lot of trust here."

Pandey Ji stood his ground, though his heart pounded in his chest. "I'm not asking for trust. I'm asking for a deal. You get what you need to take them down, and I get out of this alive."

The man considered this for a moment, then nodded slowly. "Alright. We can work with that. But know this—once this information is out, there's no going back. The owners will come after you, and they won't stop until you're dead."

Pandey Ji swallowed hard. He had known this was a possibility, but hearing it spoken aloud made it all the more real. "I understand. Just make sure it's worth it."

The man stepped forward, taking the briefcase from Pandey Ji's hand. He opened it, quickly scanning the contents. Satisfied, he closed it with a snap and looked up at Pandey Ji.

"You'll get your protection," the man said, his voice firm. "But you need to disappear—tonight. We have a safe house ready. You'll stay there until we can arrange something more permanent."

Pandey Ji nodded, feeling a strange mix of relief and dread. This was it—the moment where his old life ended and a new one began. He had made his choice, and now he had to live with it.

The man gestured for Pandey Ji to follow him to the car. As they drove away from the docks, the city lights fading into the distance, Pandey Ji couldn't help but think about everything he was leaving behind. The power, the influence, the life he had built—it was all gone now. But in its place, there was something else: a chance for redemption, a chance to finally do the right thing.

Meanwhile, back at the hotel, the owners were already making their moves. The suite that had once been a place of control and power now felt like a bunker as they gathered their most trusted associates. The atmosphere was tense, the air thick with paranoia and fear. They knew the police were closing in, and that someone had betrayed them. But they didn't know who.

"Pandey Ji is gone," one of the owners said, his voice laced with anger. "He's disappeared, and he's taken the documents with him."

The others exchanged uneasy glances. "If he hands those documents over to the police, we're finished," another owner muttered.

They quickly began making calls, pulling every string they had to locate Pandey Ji. But as the hours passed, it became clear that he had vanished without a trace. The realization sent a wave of panic through the room.

"What do we do now?" one of them asked, his voice trembling.

"We buy ourselves some time," the first owner replied, his eyes cold and calculating. "We use our connections, cover our tracks. And we wait. Eventually, he'll slip up. They always do."

But even as they plotted their next moves, a sense of dread hung over them. They had always prided themselves on being untouchable, on staying one step ahead of everyone else. But now, for the first time, they felt the ground shifting beneath their feet. The game was changing, and they weren't sure they could keep up.

At the safe house, Pandey Ji sat in a small, dimly lit room, staring out the window at the unfamiliar landscape. He had been given a new identity, new documents, a new life. But none of it felt real. The man he had been—the man who had wielded power and control with ease—was gone, replaced by someone he barely recognized.

The door creaked open, and the man who had helped him escape stepped inside. He placed a small folder on the table in front of Pandey Ji.

"This is everything you'll need," the man said. "New passport, new identification, and some cash to get you started. You'll be safe here for now, but eventually, you'll have to move on. They'll be looking for you."

Pandey Ji nodded, his fingers tracing the edge of the folder. "And the documents?"

"They're already in the right hands," the man assured him. "The police will get what they need, and the owners will be taken down. You've done your part."

Pandey Ji let out a breath he didn't realize he had been holding. It was over—or at least, his part of it was. But the cost had been high, and he wasn't sure if the victory was worth the price.

"What happens now?" Pandey Ji asked, his voice hollow.

"Now?" The man shrugged. "Now you start over. A new life, a new beginning. And maybe, if you're lucky, you'll find some peace."

Pandey Ji nodded, though he wasn't sure if peace was something he could ever achieve. Not after everything that had happened. But as he stared out the window, watching the first light of dawn break over the horizon, he allowed himself a small glimmer of hope.

For the first time in years, he had made a choice for himself. A choice that wasn't driven by fear or power, but by the desire to make things right. And maybe, just maybe, that was enough.

As he watched the sun rise, Pandey Ji knew that the road ahead would be difficult. He would have to live with the consequences of his actions, and the knowledge that he could never return to the life he had once known. But he also knew that he had done the right thing. And in the end, that was all that mattered.

The Final Gambit had been played, and now, it was time to face whatever came next.

❑❑❑

Chapter 16: The Confrontation

The morning air was crisp and still as Pratap Rao Singh made his way to the secluded part of the hotel grounds. The path was lined with tall, swaying trees, their branches casting long shadows that danced across the ground. Pratap's footsteps were quiet, yet the weight of the upcoming meeting made every step feel heavier. He had received the call from Pandey Ji only an hour ago, and though he had anticipated something like this, the reality of it had left him on edge.

Pandey Ji stood by a large oak tree, his figure partially obscured by the dense foliage. Even from a distance, Pratap could see the fear etched into the man's face. His eyes darted around nervously, as if expecting someone to leap out from the shadows at any moment. Yet beneath the fear, there was something else—determination, perhaps even defiance. Pandey Ji was a man at the end of his rope, and he had made his choice.

As Pratap approached, Pandey Ji took a deep breath, his hands trembling slightly as he extended a shaky hand toward the Inspector.

"I have information," Pandey Ji began, his voice trembling but resolute. "But you have to promise me protection. He kill me if he finds out I talked."

Pratap nodded, his expression serious. "You have my word. But you need to tell me everything, and you need to do it now."

Pandey Ji glanced around once more, then leaned in closer to Pratap, his voice dropping to a whisper and spoke into his ears.

Pratap's jaw tightened, his suspicions confirmed. He had always suspected it, but hearing it from Pandey Ji made it all the more real. He could feel the pieces of the puzzle clicking into place, the picture of Helen's murder becoming clearer with every word Pandey Ji spoke.

"I was used." Pandey Ji continued, his voice laced with bitterness. "I was the pawn. I swear, Inspector."

Pratap studied Pandey Ji's face, searching for any sign of deceit. But the man seemed genuine, his fear and guilt palpable. Pratap could see that Pandey Ji was a man caught in a web of lies and corruption, desperately trying to claw his way out.

"And now?" Pratap asked, his voice steady. "Why are you coming to me now?"

Pandey Ji swallowed hard, his eyes flicking nervously to the side. "I need your help."

Pratap nodded, understanding the man's desperation. "You did the right thing by coming to me. But I need more than just your word, Pandey Ji. I need evidence."

Pandey Ji hesitated for a moment, then reached into his coat pocket and pulled out a small flash drive. He handed it to Pratap, his hands shaking so badly that the drive almost slipped from his grasp.

"This is it," Pandey Ji whispered, his voice barely audible. "This is what she died for. Helen gathered everything—bank records, transactions, names. It's all there. If you have this, you have everything you need to bring the killer to justice."

Pratap took the flash drive, feeling the weight of it in his hand. This small piece of technology held the key to unraveling the entire operation, to bringing justice to Helen and exposing the powerful forces that had orchestrated her murder. But it also put a target on his back—a target that would only grow larger once he started using the information.

"Thank you, Pandey Ji," Pratap said, his voice firm. "You've done the right thing. Now, I need you to stay hidden. Don't talk to anyone, don't go back to the hotel."

Pandey Ji nodded, relief washing over his features. "I will, Inspector."

As Pratap made his way back to the station, his mind raced with the implications of what he had just learned. The evidence on the flash drive was damning, but it also made him a target. Pratap knew that the battle ahead would be dangerous.

Back at the station, Pratap locked himself in his office and plugged the flash drive into his computer. The files opened immediately, revealing a trove of documents that detailed every aspect of the criminal activities. Offshore accounts, shell companies, payments to corrupt officials—it was all there, meticulously documented by Helen and a video of Helen, which had more details than he had anticipated.

Pratap's heart pounded as he scrolled through the files. This was the smoking gun he had been searching for, the proof that would bring closure to the investigation.

As he pored over the documents, Pratap's phone buzzed with an incoming call. He glanced at the screen and saw that it was from his trusted colleague, Inspector Malik in Goa.

"Pratap, we've got a problem," Malik said, his voice tense.

"Word on the street is that you're not safe, Pratap. You need to get out of there. Some people are after your life."

Pratap clenched his jaw, his mind racing. He had expected retaliation, but not this quickly. The killer was moving faster than he had anticipated, and now, his life was in immediate danger.

"Thanks for the heads-up, Malik," Pratap replied, his voice steady despite the tension in his chest. "I'll take care of it."

"You better," Malik warned. "And watch your back."

Pratap ended the call and leaned back in his chair, staring at the ceiling. He knew he couldn't stay at the station any longer—it was too exposed, too vulnerable. But he also knew that he couldn't run. Not yet. He had to finish what he started, to ensure that the evidence made its way into the right hands.

He quickly backed up the files onto multiple encrypted drives and then made a series of calls to his most trusted contacts—journalists, law enforcement officials, and allies who operated outside the usual channels. He needed to spread the information far and wide, to make sure that even if something happened to him, the truth would still come out.

As night fell, Pratap left the station and made his way to a safe house that Malik had arranged for him. The location was off the grid, known only to a select few. It would buy him some time, but not much. He knew that the killer would stop at nothing to silence him.

The next morning, Pratap's phone buzzed again. This time, it was a text message from an unknown number. The message was short, but its meaning was clear.

Meet me at the warehouse. Alone. We need to talk.

Pratap stared at the message, a sense of foreboding creeping over him. The warehouse was the same place where he had met Raghav—a place that held more secrets than he cared to remember. But he knew that this was it—the final confrontation. The moment where everything would come to a head.

He replied to the message with a single word: *Understood.*

The warehouse loomed large in the distance as Pratap approached, the morning fog shrouding the building in an eerie haze. The silence was oppressive, broken only by the distant sound of waves crashing against the nearby docks. Pratap's hand hovered near his gun as he entered the building, every sense on high alert.

Inside, the air was thick with tension. The shadows seemed to move, shifting with every step Pratap took. And then he saw them, the very familiar faces, standing in a semi-circle near the center of the warehouse. Their faces were grim, their eyes cold and calculating. They were flanked by a group of enforcers, each one armed and ready for violence.

"Inspector Pratap Rao Singh," the leader said, his voice dripping with disdain. "You've caused us a great deal of trouble."

Pratap met the man's gaze, his own expression steely. "I could say the same about you."

His eyes glinted with malice. "You're a fool if you think you can win this. I control everything—every cop, every judge, every politician. You're nothing but a speck of dust in our path."

Pratap's hand tightened on his gun, but he didn't draw it. Not yet. "Maybe," he said calmly. "But I have something you don't."

"And what might that be?"

Pratap's eyes locked onto the person. "The truth. And evidence to back it up."

For a moment, there was silence in the warehouse, the weight of Pratap's words hanging in the air. It is replaced by a flicker of doubt. But it was quickly masked by a cold, calculated expression.

"You think evidence matters?" His voice was low and dangerous. "You think you can take us down with some files? We own this city, Inspector. We own everything."

Pratap remained calm, his gaze never vanished.. "Maybe you do. But I've already sent copies of that evidence to people you can't control. Journalists, law enforcement, people who care more about justice than money. By now, it's already out of your hands."

NOW The OWNER's face twisted into a snarl, his composure slipping. "You're lying."

Pratap shook his head. "You can't stop it. It's too late."

The tension in the warehouse reached a boiling point. The enforcers shifted uneasily, their hands twitching near their weapons. Pratap could feel the danger in the air, the threat of violence looming just beneath the surface. But he stood his ground, knowing that this was the moment everything had been leading to.

The lead owner stepped forward, his voice a deadly whisper. "You think you're clever, don't you, Inspector? But you're just a man—a man who's about to find out what happens when you cross the wrong people."

Pratap's hand moved to his gun, his instincts screaming at him to be ready. "Maybe. But I'm not alone."

At that moment, the doors to the warehouse burst open, and a squad of police officers stormed in, their weapons drawn. Pratap's backup had arrived, just as he had planned. The enforcers raised their weapons, but they were quickly surrounded, outnumbered and outgunned.

The lead owner's face went pale as he realized that the tables had turned. "You… you set us up."

Pratap nodded, his voice steady. "You're under arrest. All of you. For the murder of Helen D'Souza, for money laundering, for corruption. It's over."

The owner looked around desperately, but there was no escape. The police closed in, and the enforcers were quickly disarmed and taken into custody. The owners, once so powerful and untouchable, were now just criminals facing justice.

As the police led the owners away in handcuffs, Pratap felt a wave of relief wash over him. It was finally over. The conspiracy that had taken Helen's life, that had threatened to destroy everything, had been brought down.

But even as the dust settled, Pratap knew that the fight wasn't completely over. There would be trials, investigations, and no doubt more battles ahead. But for now, he had won. And Helen's death had not been in vain.

Later that evening, Pratap stood on the rooftop of his apartment, watching the city lights twinkle in the distance. The wind was cool against his skin, and for the first time in days, he allowed himself to breathe deeply, to feel the weight of the case lifting from his shoulders.

His phone buzzed with a message from Malik. *Good job, Pratap. You did it.*

Pratap smiled faintly as he replied. *We did it. Thanks for having my back.*

As he put his phone away, Pratap looked out at the city again, his thoughts turning to Helen. She had been brave, determined to expose the truth no matter the cost. And though she hadn't lived to see justice served, her efforts had made all the difference.

Pratap knew that there would be more cases, more challenges ahead. But for now, he could rest, knowing that he had done everything he could to make things right.

And that, he decided, was enough.

❑❑❑

Chapter 17: Justice Served

The aftermath of the sting was a whirlwind of chaos and revelation. Within hours of the arrests, the media exploded with the story—a tale of corporate corruption, money laundering, and murder that sent shockwaves through the city. News channels and newspapers plastered the faces of the once-powerful owners across their headlines, exposing the depths of their criminal activities. The scandal was unprecedented, and it left the entire corporate world reeling.

Pratap Rao Singh stood at the edge of the police cordon, watching as the last of the suspects were taken away in the back of a police van. The early morning light bathed the scene in a soft glow, but there was nothing peaceful about the aftermath of the operation. The weight of what had transpired hung heavy in the air, a reminder of the dark deeds that had finally been brought to light.

As the van's doors slammed shut, Pratap allowed himself a moment of reflection. The case had been one of the most challenging of his career, filled with twists and turns that had tested his resolve at every step. But now, as the sun began to rise over the city, he felt a sense of closure. Justice had been served, and Helen's death, though tragic, had not been in vain.

He was pulled from his thoughts by the sound of footsteps approaching. It was Aniruddh Pant, looking weary but relieved. The General Manager had been through the wringer—interrogations, accusations, and the crushing weight of guilt. Yet, despite his involvement in the affair, he had been cleared of murder charges. The evidence had shown that while Aniruddh had been complicit in the company's illegal activities, he had not been directly involved in Helen's death.

"Inspector," Aniruddh greeted Pratap, his voice tinged with exhaustion. "I just wanted to thank you… for everything."

Pratap turned to face him, his expression unreadable. "Thank me? You were part of this, Aniruddh. You may not have killed Helen, but you helped create the environment that led to her death."

Aniruddh nodded, his shoulders slumping. "I know. And I'll have to live with that for the rest of my life. But I'm trying to make things right. I've resigned from my position, and I'm leaving the corporate world behind. It's the least I can do."

Pratap studied him for a moment, searching for any sign of deception. But all he saw was a man who had been broken by his own choices, now trying to pick up the pieces of his shattered life.

"Do you think leaving will make up for what you've done?" Pratap asked, his tone firm but not unkind.

Aniruddh shook his head. "No. But it's a start. I don't know if I can ever atone for my mistakes, but I have to try. I have to believe that it's not too late to change."

Pratap nodded slowly, his gaze softening. "It's never too late to do the right thing, Aniruddh. But don't think for a moment that leaving absolves you of your responsibility. You'll carry this with you, wherever you go."

"I know," Aniruddh whispered, his voice thick with emotion. "I just hope… I hope I can find a way to live with it."

Pratap watched as Aniruddh turned and walked away, his figure disappearing into the bustling crowd of reporters and onlookers. The man was a shadow of his former self, but perhaps, in his fall from grace, he had found a sliver of redemption. Only time would tell.

Pandey Ji, too, had faced the consequences of his actions. Though directly involved in the crime, he had been granted limited leniency in exchange for his cooperation with the police. His testimony had been crucial in bringing down the owners and he was ordered to serve 14 years imprisonment.

Pratap had watched as Pandey Ji packed up his belongings, the weight of his decision evident in every movement. The man who had once wielded power and influence within the company was now a shadow of his former self, haunted by the choices he had made and the lives he had destroyed.

Their final conversation had been brief, but it had carried the weight of everything that had transpired.

"Where will you go?" Pratap had asked as Pandey Ji prepared to leave.

"Somewhere far from here," Pandey Ji had replied, his voice hollow. "Somewhere I can try to forget."

"You can't forget, Pandey Ji," Pratap had said, his tone gentle but firm. "You can only learn to live with it. But maybe... maybe you can find a way to make amends."

Pandey Ji had nodded, though his expression remained troubled. "I hope so, Inspector. I hope so."

And with that, Pandey Ji had left, disappearing into the distance as he sought to escape the shadows that had haunted him for so long. Whether he would find peace was a question that only time could answer.

As for Pratap Rao Singh, he stood alone in the early morning light, watching as the city slowly came to life around him. The case was over, but the memories of what had transpired lingered in his mind. Helen's death had brought to light a web of deceit and corruption that might have otherwise remained hidden. The owners had been taken down, but the scars they had left behind would take time to heal.

Pratap's phone buzzed in his pocket, pulling him from his thoughts. It was a message from his trusted colleague, Inspector Malik.

"You did it, Pratap. Justice served. Proud of you, my friend. But I still have some doubts. We can discuss when we meet. Did the owners kill Helen, or was it by an accident?"

Pratap smiled faintly as he read the message, but the sense of closure he sought remained elusive. He knew that the fight for justice was never truly done. There would always be more cases, more battles to fight, and more people in need of protection. But for now, he could rest knowing that he had done his job.

He recollects Pandey ji's statements, which he whispered to his ears.

"Sir, Helen was a nice girl. Yes, she was into the trap and wanted to take revenge. Being close to owners, she has access to everything. And she wanted money as well by selling company data. She was caught and blackmailed after that in multiple ways. She wanted to kill them. But they were too smart. They got to know before hand and wanted to kill her. The plan was made and poison was arranged.

They wanted to use me and my research head to become a puppet in case they were caught. Since there was a lot of family pressure at Helen's end, another possibility was to declare death suicide attempt or accidental consumption of deadly poison. She was diabetic and I poisioned her through the lancet of the glocumeter. If I would not have said yes, probably Shyam might have said yes. He wanted money for his family as well. Bone marrow to be arranged. Huge money required. John Hoppkins is very costly. 1 Cr you know.

Owners wanted to use me and I was under compulsion." Pandey looked at Pratap.

'Why would Helen do so?' Pratap asked.

'Videos of Helen Sir. They were blackmailing her every passing day. Even once in front of me. But destiny had some different plans. She wanted money to make her mother get cured. Initially she wanted some good amount from the owners. Later she was trapped.'

He looked out over the city, the sun rising higher in the sky, casting its warm light over the buildings and streets below. It was a new day, and with it came the promise of new challenges. But Pratap was ready. He had faced the darkness, and he had emerged on the other side, stronger and more determined than ever. Hellen has got due justice. Punishment to Pandey and Owners were established.

As he turned to leave, his thoughts lingered on Helen. She had been a brave woman, determined to expose the truth no matter the cost. And though her life had been cut short, her legacy would live on. Her death had not been in vain.

Pratap Rao Singh walked away from the scene, his footsteps steady and sure. The case was closed, but the fight for justice continued. And he would be there, every step of the way, ready to face whatever came next.

❑❑❑

Printed in Great Britain
by Amazon

58640836R00116